## She Loved Nick.

The idea astounded her. She didn't even know *how* to love, perhaps because she'd never been truly loved. Yet there was no doubt. She was definitely in love with Nick.

Right from the first, the signs had been there—all of them in big, bright, red neon letters. How could she have missed them?

There was the way he'd mesmerized her on the night of her birthday and the way her body had melted against his when they'd danced. There was the way she'd so easily acquiesced to the idea of flying to some unknown destination for dinner and the stunning fact that she'd turned down Des's offer for her.

Drops of rain began to fall. She didn't care.

The rain was cool. Her skin was hot. She wanted Nick.

Dear Reader,

Welcome to Silhouette Desire—where you're guaranteed powerful, passionate and provocative love stories that feature rugged heroes and spirited heroines who experience the full emotional intensity of falling in love!

Wonderful and ever-popular Annette Broadrick brings us September's MAN OF THE MONTH with *Lean, Mean & Lonesome.* Watch as a tough loner returns home to face the woman he walked away from but never forgot.

Our exciting continuity series TEXAS CATTLEMAN'S CLUB continues with *Cinderella's Tycoon* by Caroline Cross. Charismatic CEO Sterling Churchill marries a shy librarian pregnant with his sperm-bank baby—and finds love.

*Proposition: Marriage* is what rising star Eileen Wilks offers when the girl-next-door comes alive in the arms of an alpha hero. Beloved romance author Fayrene Preston makes her Desire debut with *The Barons of Texas: Tess,* featuring a beautiful heiress who falls in love with a sexy stranger. The popular theme BACHELORS & BABIES returns to Desire with Metsy Hingle's *Dad in Demand.* And Barbara McCauley's miniseries SECRETS! continues with the dramatic story of a mysterious millionaire in *Killian's Passion.*

So make a commitment to sensual love—treat yourself to all six September love stories from Silhouette Desire!

Enjoy!

Joan Marlow Golan
Senior Editor, Silhouette Desire

---

Please address questions and book requests to:
Silhouette Reader Service
U.S.: 3010 Walden Ave., P.O. Box 1325, Buffalo, NY 14269
Canadian: P.O. Box 609, Fort Erie, Ont. L2A 5X3

# THE BARONS OF TEXAS: TESS
## FAYRENE PRESTON

SILHOUETTE Desire®

Published by Silhouette Books

America's Publisher of Contemporary Romance

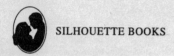 SILHOUETTE BOOKS

ISBN 0-373-76240-2

THE BARONS OF TEXAS: TESS

Copyright © 1999 by Fayrene Preston

Visit us at www.romance.net

**Printed in U.S.A.**

## FAYRENE PRESTON

published her first book in 1981 and has been publishing steadily ever since. *The Barons of Texas: Tess* is her first novel for Silhouette Books, and she is delighted to be on board. Fayrene lives in north Texas and is the mother of two grown sons. She claims her greatest achievement in life is turning out two wonderful human beings. She is also proud to announce the arrival of her first grandchild: a beautiful baby girl. Now she has even more to be thankful for.

This book is dedicated
with many, many thanks to:

R. G. Font, Ph.D., CPG, PG,
EurGeol President, Geoscience Data Management

# One

Tall, lean and bronzed, the man stood at the edge of the terrace watching her, just as he had for the last fifteen minutes. Tess Baron tried to ignore him and focus instead on her party guests, but she found it virtually impossible.

Something about his stillness compelled her attention. It was like lightning caught in a bottle, an electric tension that would be safe only as long as it was contained. And he didn't strike her as the type of man to contain his energies for long.

This was her birthday party. She knew everyone here. Everyone, that was, except *him*.

She skimmed the crowd, wondering who had brought him, but everyone was either dancing or mixing. No one looked as if they'd brought a guest, then forgotten him. Besides, she reflected ruefully, it would be impossible to forget him.

Behind him, the sun was slowly setting into the Gulf of

Mexico, its great orange ball searing the water with its heat as it dipped lower and lower. Silhouetted against the elemental tableau, with the sun surrounding him, the man looked larger than life—a sun god.

At that moment she wouldn't have bet money against the possibility that he had lassoed the sun down from the sky.

She exhaled a long breath, reminded herself that she didn't have a quixotic bone in her body, and forced her focus elsewhere. At least everything else about her party was going well.

A warm breeze from off the Gulf waters somehow matched the band's sensual bossa nova beat. Icy margaritas and long neck beers were being served, along with mounds of jumbo Gulf shrimp and oysters harvested fresh that day. Out on the lawn, barbecued *cabrito* turned on a spit.

*He* ate or drank nothing, though she'd seen waiters offering him his preference of drinks.

"Happy birthday, Tess."

The voice of a longtime friend snapped her mind back to her party. "Thanks, Becca." She kissed the cheek of the pretty young woman, then reached up to hug Becca's college sweetheart and husband, Mel Grant. "I'm so glad you two could come."

Becca laughed. "Are you kidding? Your birthday parties are way too much fun to miss. Besides, Corpus Christi is a pretty cool city."

Mel smiled at her. "It's become a party game to try to guess where you're going to hold your parties each year. The year you threw your party in Kuala Lumpur is now legendary. But last year I felt a little let down."

She grinned. "Oh, yeah?"

"*Southfork?*" He shook his head. "Not very original, Tess, and way too close to home."

She laughed. "Sorry, but the location of my parties depends on where I'm working, and last year I was working at home.''

"I know, but personally, I was hoping for an oil rig in the South China Sea.''

"An oil rig is no place to throw a party—*which* you very well know. Too much chance for harm on either side.''

Mel worked for Coastal Petroleum, one of the world's major oil companies. Nevertheless, he sighed dramatically. "Okay, okay, I'll give you that, plus a big thumbs-up for this year.''

"What a relief," she said dryly.

"Yep. This is a great house, right on the beach and with a fabulous view. I'd say you made up the points you lost last year.''

"Ignore him, Tess," Becca advised.

"He's much too entertaining to ignore. Besides, he's right. This is a great house. I leased it because my new offshore drilling site is straight out there.'' She pointed toward the Gulf. "And because there's a great helipad at the side of the house.''

Mel nodded. "By the way, congratulations. Word is you think the reservoir you've found out there will be your richest oil discovery yet.''

She grimaced, and her hand automatically went to cover her stomach, where a heavy dread appeared every time she thought of what she was gambling on this one site. "Do me a favor and don't congratulate me yet. I'm superstitious. The initial tests were very encouraging, but in the end, we both know that could mean nothing. I won't celebrate until we strike that first oil and the well actually starts to produce.''

Becca waved a dismissive hand. "You're like a bloodhound when it comes to oil. I'd back your instincts before I would all those sophisticated tests they do. If you like what you've seen out there, then the oil is as good as in the pipeline.''

Tess gave Becca a quick, grateful hug. ''Thank you.''

Her instincts had always been solid; Becca was right about that. Yet the stakes were so high on this particular venture that she couldn't be sure her instincts hadn't been tainted by her need for this well to come in big, not to mention quick.

''Word is also out that you've been having some problems,'' Mel continued. ''In case you decide you need some help, just remember, my company is always interested.''

Unfortunately, it was very hard to keep secrets in the oil business. ''You know how I feel about my oil ventures, Mel.''

''I know, I know. They're your babies, and you keep them until they're raised and well into old age.''

She nodded. ''It's a family tradition.'' She'd hoped this party would help her relax and have a good time, something she hadn't been able to do in a long time. Unfortunately, though, her nerves were tighter than ever. Between Mel and his well-meaning talk of her problems and the *man*... He hadn't moved, and he was still looking at her with that laser gaze of his. Beneath his stare, her skin felt just like it was being sunburned.

''Listen, do either of you know that man standing over there, leaning against the balustrade?''

Both Becca and Mel glanced over their shoulders. ''No, but if I weren't with Mel tonight, I would *love* to.''

Mel frowned at his wife. ''Excuse me, but I don't think that's funny.''

''No?'' With her eyes twinkling with laughter, she reached for her husband's hand. ''Then how about dancing with me? Maybe it will come back to me why I love you so much.''

"That sounds like a challenge and I'm definitely up for it." With a wink at Tess, he pulled his wife onto the dance floor. "See you later."

"You bet." Surely there was a simple explanation for the man's presence. Tess pondered. One of her guests must have brought him, but if so, why weren't they with him? Why hadn't they introduced him to her? And most of all, why did he keep looking at her?

*And*, damn it, where was Ron? He might be able to tell her the identity of the man. Ron Hughes was a bright, competent young man in his late twenties. As her assistant, it was his job to know everything and everyone, and he usually did. But he was probably still in the house, working in the two-room suite they'd appropriated as their offices for the time they would be there.

Someone lightly clasped her elbow. "Dance?"

She started, then inwardly laughed at herself. No, she reflected wryly, there was nothing at all wrong with her nerves. She looked around. "Colin! Oh, great, you made it."

"Did you doubt it for a minute?"

She smiled. "No."

Colin Wynne, tanned, suave and incredibly good-looking, was one of Dallas's most eligible bachelors. He was also one of her favorite people, though they'd never dated. She'd never had the desire to go out with him other than in a group, and she knew the feeling was mutual. Over the years, she'd found friendships to be much more satisfying than a love life. He held out his hand to her.

"Thanks," she said, "but not right now. I still have some details to see to. The party's really just beginning."

"Nonsense. I'm here. You're here. The party has officially started."

She grinned. Few people possessed the self-confidence

Colin did. He made everything he did look easy, yet he was one of the hardest-working people she knew. "Who did you bring tonight?"

"I didn't bring a date, if that's what you mean—just a planeload of the usual suspects."

"Oh, that's right. I heard you were going to fly down some of the group in your new jet. Thanks."

"No problem at all."

She leaned closer to him. "Do you know that man standing over there by the edge of the terrace?"

He threw a casual glance over his shoulder. "Nope. Who is he? A party crasher?"

She shook her head. "He must have come with someone. I just can't figure out who yet."

"You want me to go over and check him out?"

"No. I'll do it in a minute."

"Happy birthday, Tess." A cool voice slipped between them and they both turned.

"Jill." She gave her sister a quick, automatic hug. If the hug lacked the spontaneity and ease of the hug she'd given Becca, she prided herself on her belief that no one could tell. No one except maybe Jill. And Colin, who knew them both well.

Just as quickly, she released her middle sister and stepped back. Jill was wearing a short black Armani sheath that emphasized her inherent elegance and sophistication. Until Tess had seen Jill, she'd thought she looked pretty good in her short, ivory silk dress with straps that skimmed over her shoulders and crisscrossed several times in the back until reaching her waist.

But then, it was Jill who had inherited the classical beauty and elegance of their mother, not her nor Kit. Even Jill's dark hair was styled into an elaborate French twist from which no hair would dare escape.

Annoyingly, Tess could feel the wind blowing at the untidy blond tendrils of her hair, which had already managed to elude the containment of the ivory silk scarf she'd tied at the nape of her neck. "You're late. What happened? I expected you earlier."

"My ride took off without me, and I had to make other arrangements to get here." Jill's bourbon-colored gaze flashed at Colin.

The very picture of innocence, he spread out his hands. "I had a schedule to meet."

"You weren't running a bus, Colin." Jill's words dripped with ice. "You were flying your own plane."

"Ever heard of a little thing called a flight plan?"

"Yes, as a matter of fact, I have. And I know they can give you a certain leeway."

He shrugged. "Everyone else was aboard. I didn't see why they should be punished just because you couldn't arrange your day so you could get to the airport on time."

Tess rolled her eyes, though neither Jill nor Colin saw her, so intent were they on squaring off against each other. But she'd grown used to their behavior. For whatever reason, whenever the two of them got together, some type of sparks usually flew, and more often than not, it was sparks of anger.

"I have an idea," she said. "Why don't you two go dance and I'll see you both later?"

Colin looked at her, then at Jill. After a moment, he slowly held out his hand to her. Jill hesitated for several seconds, then glanced at Tess. "Have Uncle William and Des arrived yet?"

"Uncle William isn't feeling well, so he won't be coming."

Jill's perfect forehead creased in a frown. "Is it serious?"

Colin dropped his hand.

"He didn't give me any reason to believe that it was. Besides, you know Des would let us know if something was seriously wrong."

Jill nodded. "What about Des?"

Good question, Tess thought wryly. It was the eternal question that kept her and her sisters occupied. "I have no idea if he's even coming."

"You haven't heard from him?"

"You know he rarely lets us know what he's up to."

"Right." Jill chewed her bottom lip for perhaps three seconds, then stopped. It was a habit left over from her childhood. "Well, let me know if Des arrives, okay?"

Sure she would, Tess thought. When pigs flew.

Jill switched her attention to Colin. "Well?"

"Well, what, Jill?"

"Do you or don't you want to dance?"

This time it was Colin who hesitated. "Maybe later," he finally said and walked off.

Tess hid a smile. If looks could kill, Colin would now be dead. Jill stared after him for a moment longer, then turned and went in the opposite direction.

The Des in whom Jill had been so interested was their uncle William's elusive stepson, a high-powered lawyer. Women flocked to Des like bees to honey, but he was much more than a highly eligible bachelor to her and her two sisters. She, Jill and Kit had each inherited one-sixth of their family's business upon the death of their father, conditional upon each of them meeting a certain criterion. But Des was due to inherit fifty percent of their family company upon Uncle William's death.

That fact put Des smack in the center of the collective crosshairs of her and her sisters. In theory, if one of them married him, they would gain control of the family com-

pany. And there wasn't one of them who wasn't hungry for
that control and more than willing, able and raring to go
after him. Too bad for her sisters that *she* planned to be the
one who got him.

However, pursuing Des was frustrating as hell. Though
she was no expert on love, it seemed to her that the only
way to get Des to fall in love with her was to arrange it so
that they could spend time with each other. But time was
something Des rarely gave any of them on an individual
basis.

Still, she wasn't deterred, nor, she knew, were her sisters.
Winning control of the company was too important for each
of them. If Des showed up tonight, Jill would go after him
like a heat-seeking missile, but she would have to stand in
line behind Tess. And then, of course, there was Kit.

The three of them had been competitive with each other
since birth, encouraged and egged on by their father, who
pounded into each of them the importance of being the best
at whatever they did. One of their competitions involved
fighting to be the one who, at the end of the company's
fiscal year, had made the most money for the company, and
there wasn't much they wouldn't do to earn that yearly
honor. *Or* to win Des's agreement to marriage.

But this year, she, even more than Kit and Jill, had a
tremendous amount to prove.

"Dance with me."

She looked up and took a reflexive step backward. She'd
been so lost in the dysfunctional dynamics of her family
that she'd momentarily forgotten her unknown guest. Now
he was standing in front of her, tall, broad-shouldered and
a bit overpowering.

And his eyes, she finally saw, were a startling amber.

"Who are you?"

"Someone who would like very much to dance with you."

His voice reverberated deep inside her, warm and compelling, like a playful silken ribbon that dipped and curved throughout her, making her heart pound like a bass drum.

His amber eyes held her gaze. His name. She didn't know his name.

It didn't matter.

He took her hand, and suddenly she found herself on the dance floor, and she wasn't entirely certain how she'd gotten there. Surely she'd told him no.

Apparently not.

His arms were strong as they held her to his hard body. His dance steps were smooth, so that following him was easy, which allowed her to register other things. Such as the heat his body generated—it had the power to melt an iceberg.

This was a man who was definitely confident with his own sexuality and did nothing to hold it back. In addition, those amber eyes of his held dark, intriguing depths she hadn't expected. And his skin was bronzed to a beautiful golden brown that made her think he must spend a great deal of time outdoors. His dark brown hair was almost outshone by streaks that could only have been put there by the brightness of the sun.

Truly he *could* be a sun god.

If she believed in such things.

Still, all her instincts were shouting at her that she would be safer if she simply walked away from him. There was just one problem. She wasn't certain she could. His body had suddenly become her own private universe's center of gravity.

Thankfully, she could still think, and truthfully, she was

way too curious to attempt to leave him at this point. "Were you invited to my party?"

"No."

Just the single word. No explanation, as if none was needed. "Did you come with one of my guests?"

"No."

A shiver raced down her spine. He was studying her as if she were a book he was trying to learn, yet he wasn't asking any questions. He was leaving that to her.

"Then why are you here?"

"Because of you." His voice was soft, yet intense and with a faint trace of some dark emotion. "You're really quite beautiful, you know. I didn't expect it."

"You didn't...?"

He slowly shook his head, his gaze never once leaving her.

She found herself speechless. She felt as if he'd isolated her from the rest of the world, yet she was surrounded by friends, none of whom seemed the least bit alarmed that she was dancing with a perfect stranger who radiated a barely contained electric energy and thus danger.

But then, they couldn't see what she was seeing, nor could they feel what he was making her feel.

A dark fire simmered in the depths of his remarkable eyes—eyes, she was convinced, that, if he chose, he could use like a lethal weapon. With a single glance he would be able to mow down anyone who got in his way or, conversely, reach across the terrace and touch her, making her aware of him in every part of her body. And that had been when they were yards from each other.

Now, as she danced with him, he was having an even greater impact on her. She couldn't have said what the band was playing. She only knew that the two of them were moving slowly, sensually and in perfect unison. And, oddly, it seemed very right.

Her reaction didn't make sense.

*He* didn't make sense.

The sun had almost set, leaving behind fading streaks of red, orange and gold just above the horizon. The lights around the dance floor and in the trees had come on, yet he remained every bit as powerful, as elemental and as comfortable as he had been with the sun behind him.

"Happy birthday, Tess," someone called.

"Thank you," she said, blindly glancing in the direction of the voice, then immediately looked back at him, the man whose heat had melted her and whose strength had molded her against him with ease. Her breasts were pressed against his chest, her legs rubbed against the steel of his thighs. She didn't even know his name, yet the aggressive, masculine force of his body impacted her every cell, bringing out feminine urges and needs so new, she wasn't sure what to do with them.

"You throw a great party," he murmured.

"Thank you. It was so good of you to come."

For the first time he smiled at her—a partial smile, a knowing smile, a completely self-assured smile. And the effect was a shock of electricity that bolted straight through her and made her catch her breath. A full smile from him might stop her heart.

Her hand moved restlessly over his shoulder, the fine cut and expensive cloth of his dark suit adding one more piece to the puzzle of him. Simply by dancing with him, she was coming to know his body well, and she could tell his strength didn't come from bulky muscles but rather the lean, elongated muscles of a natural athlete. Yet another piece. "Do you make it a practice to crash parties?"

"Actually, this is my first."

"And are you having a good time?"

"So far I can't complain."

"If you'll tell me your name, I might put you on the guest list for next year. Or would you just prefer to crash again?"

"Neither. I'm afraid I can't wait a year to see you again."

"Why—" Someone bumped against her back. Protectively, he tightened his hold on her and circled her in another direction.

"Hey, Sis. Happy birthday."

She looked around, then inwardly sighed. She should have known. No one but her youngest sister, Kit, would deliberately bump into her. And no one but Kit would have dressed for what she knew to be a dressy affair in a tight T-shirt, even tighter jeans and a pair of Western boots that Tess knew for a fact were eight years old and looked twelve. "Thank you."

The man didn't relinquish his hold on her, but he did allow room for her to turn toward her sister.

"Is Des coming?" Kit asked, all the while doing some sort of dance that amazingly fit the music.

Kit's red hair was flying; her green eyes were sparkling. Her arms were in the air, and her hips and feet were moving in a way that not only looked incredibly sexy but made Tess feel a tinge of envy that Kit could move so uninhibitedly. Kit's partner was someone she didn't know, but from the looks of his jeans, Western-cut shirt and boots, she guessed he might be a new hire at the family ranch.

"I don't know. Des didn't RSVP."

Kit came to an abrupt stop, though her partner didn't seem to notice and kept on dancing. "Des couldn't be more exasperating if he tried, and I sometimes suspect he does."

"You got it."

Tess knew that Kit's aim in bringing one of the ranch hands to her party and dressing like she had almost every day of her life since she'd gotten out of diapers was to flout tradition and embarrass her sisters. But what Kit didn't realize was that she looked better in her jeans and T-shirt than half the women at the party whose dresses had come from Neiman Marcus. And a cursory glance at the crowd showed her that at least three of her single friends and two of the married ones were openly salivating over Kit's date.

Kit hooked her thumbs in her pockets and flashed Tess's dance partner a smile that revealed a perfect set of dimples. "Who's your date, Sis?"

"I haven't the slightest idea."

Kit's eyebrows rose. "Cool," she said, her tone for once sincere. Then she danced away.

The man laughed, a deep chuckle.

Drawing away from him, she looked at him. "Is there some reason you won't tell me your name? Like maybe you're at the top of the FBI's Most Wanted list?"

"No."

"Then tell me."

He shrugged. "The thing is, I doubt my name will mean anything to you."

She exhaled a long breath, reaching for patience. "Why don't you let me decide that? I'm tired of this little game you're playing. Tell me or I'm going to walk away."

A slow smile spread across his face, this smile even more powerful than his last. "Ah...a threat from the birthday girl."

She refused to be affected by his smile, though she could feel the futility of her resistance as it slipped by the moment. "Are you or are you not going to tell me?"

"Nick Trejo. My name is Nick Trejo."

The name sounded vaguely familiar, but for the life of

her, she couldn't place it. "Okay, you're right. It doesn't mean anything to me."

"I didn't think it would."

"Uh-huh. Okay. Let me try another tack. How did you know about this party tonight?"

"I've made it my business to find out as much as possible about you."

Suddenly cautious, she stared at him, wondering if she could figure him out if she stared at him long enough. But no. He wasn't giving anything away—not by expression, and certainly not by words.

"Don't worry. I'm not a stalker."

"No? Then, Nick Trejo, I think it's past time you told me what you want."

"That's easy," he said, pulling her against him while his amber gaze held steady on her. "I want peace on earth, food and shelter enough for every living being, but right now I'm satisfied just to be dancing with you." His voice turned raspy. "You feel good against me. You *fit* me."

One minute he had her regarding him with caution, the next he had her melting with heat. And she couldn't very well protest or say she didn't understand what he was saying, since from the beginning of their dance, her body had involuntarily molded itself to his and there had been nothing she could do about it.

One song had stopped. Another had begun. An intimate cloud of music settled around the party and mingled with the night's scents to mesmerize, tantalize. But it all paled in comparison to him.

"Did I tell you that you look beautiful?"

She couldn't remember if he had or not. In fact, she was having trouble remembering anything. It was as if he had taken her over, body, mind and soul. She wasn't used to being called beautiful, and she certainly had never thought of herself that way. Not with Jill as a sister.

Abruptly, she tore herself from his arms. "I need something to drink."

"It's your party," he said mildly. "I imagine you can have anything you want."

"You're right." Fully aware that he was following her, she threaded her way through the dancers, a smile pasted on her face for her friends, but barely acknowledging their comments.

"A shot of whiskey with a beer chaser, please," she told the bartender as soon as she reached the bar. It was a unique request for her, but tonight she felt the need for something stronger than her usual beer. She glanced at Nick. "What would you like?"

"Since I'm not an official guest at the party, I wouldn't presume."

She gave a short laugh. "More than you have already, you mean? Give me a break. You've already crashed the party. What's one drink?" She glanced at the bartender. "Give him the same thing, please." She couldn't see a man like Nick Trejo drinking anything else, certainly not the margaritas that were flowing more freely than water tonight.

Nick shook his head at the bartender, then returned his gaze to her. "I hate to tell you this, Tess, but I truly haven't yet started to presume. Believe me when I say you'll know when I do."

Jill walked to the bar. "A margarita, please. Tess, have you heard anything from Des since we last talked?"

"*No.*" She'd been dealing with Nick, trying to retain her mental balance while she played his guessing game. At the same time, she'd been fighting to keep her body from completely betraying how much she had enjoyed being held against him. And it had all taken more out of her than she had realized, leaving her with zero patience for Jill and her preoccupation with landing Des.

"Okay." Jill threw an assessing gaze at Nick, then at her. "I think I'll try to locate him by phone."

"Fine. Do that. And be sure to mention how much I've missed him tonight." Even though she knew Jill would ignore her request, she'd thrown it in to nettle her sister.

For the first time in what seemed hours, she forced herself to draw a deep breath and look away from Nick. A quick assessment of her party showed her that it was going strong, but she caught several surreptitious glances from some of her closer friends, and she knew why. They'd never before seen her allow one man to monopolize her time as she had with Nick. Except there had been no *allowing* on her part. He was like a force that she had no defenses against. It was past time she rectified that.

The bartender placed her requested shot of whiskey and mug of beer in front of her. She picked up the whiskey, but sipped.

"Okay, Nick, I'm ready to admit it. You've got me completely baffled. Why on earth do you want to see me and why here? If it's about business—and it must be, since we haven't met before tonight, and you've assured me you aren't a stalker—why didn't you simply call my office and make an appointment?"

"Let's step away from the bar," Nick murmured, taking the shot glass from her and setting it on the bar. Then, with his hand at her elbow, he led her to a less populated area of the terrace. And she went with him, telling herself it was because she was curious and not because she couldn't refuse him.

When they reached a corner of the terrace where a profusion of sweet-scented Maid of Orleans star-flowered jasmine grew, Nick turned to her. "I tried for weeks to get an appointment with you, Tess, and couldn't get one."

"Who did you talk to?"

"Your assistant, Ron Hughes. Actually, I spoke with him on almost a daily basis, but he would never put me through to you or even give me an appointment. He kept insisting you had no time to see me."

She shrugged. "Well, that's true. My schedule is always packed, especially lately, with the details for my new off-shore venture." Normally she wouldn't tell someone who was practically a stranger the reason she was busy, but something told her Nick already knew the reason. Her curiosity grew stronger. "Still, I notice Ron couldn't stop you from getting to me."

"That would have been hard for anyone to do."

She could only stare. If he'd looked amazing with the sun surrounding him, he looked astounding by moonlight. The moon's silver light threaded its way through his sun-streaked hair and touched his bronzed skin, cooling down his coloring—in a way, gentling it. Perhaps someone less suspecting than she would, at first glance, think him tame.

She knew better.

The moon might be offering him camouflage, and at the moment he might be masterfully controlling his innate power, but his amber eyes still held the intensity that earlier that evening had been able to reach across the terrace to her. She had no doubt that, if he chose, he could sear layers from her skin with just a glance.

"What's so important to you? What did you tell Ron you wanted to see me about?"

His gaze was level, his tone assured. "I wanted to ask you to stop your drilling as soon as possible."

She couldn't help it—she laughed. "No *wonder* he turned you down. Such a request is preposterous."

A muscle jumped in his cheek. "From most people, maybe. But then you and I aren't most people, and you haven't heard my reasons yet."

She didn't think she'd ever heard anything as ludicrous as his request. Obviously he knew nothing about the oil business and even less about her business dealings. "It doesn't matter what your reasons are. There's no way I'll stop."

He surprised her then. With another one of his slight smiles, he circled her throat with his fingers and stroked her skin with his thumb in an almost casual manner that completely derailed her thoughts. "You're a very ambitious woman, Tess Baron, but somehow, I think I have a chance to change your mind."

"You're crazy," she whispered, as the heat from his touch backed up in her lungs.

"Maybe, but will you at least give me a chance to explain what my reasons are?"

"I—I can't. The party—"

"Not tonight. Tomorrow. I'll meet you for breakfast, wherever and whenever you say."

She'd known him for only a short time, but she already knew that saying no to him would do no good. If nothing else, his actions tonight had showed her that he was determined to give her an explanation of some sort. *Plus,* there was an annoying feeling of excitement inside her building at the prospect of getting to see him again. "Okay. Tomorrow morning for breakfast. Here at nine."

"Good," he said softly, his hand still at her neck, his long fingers moving up and down her throat. "Very good." Then he bent his head and kissed her, slowly, as if he had all the time in the world, and thoroughly, devouring her taste as if he wanted to make it a part of him so that he could take it with him. By the time he lifted his head, she had to reach out for the terrace balustrade in order not to fall.

"I'll see you tomorrow morning."

She could only nod and watch as he slipped through an opening in the terrace railing and disappeared into the night.

Gradually and with great effort she pulled herself together. Once her breathing had evened and her pulse had steadied, she returned to the bar and downed the rest of her whiskey. Ignoring the beer, she ordered a large margarita. With it firmly in her hand, she rejoined her party.

Around four in the morning, when the last of her guests had either left or gone to their rooms, and she'd had way more margaritas than she should have, she slipped into her bed. And she couldn't help but wonder what would happen in five hours when she saw Nick Trejo again.

Why was he so sure he could convince her to stop drilling? Then again, his reason didn't really matter. He was wrong. There was nothing more important to her than striking oil as soon as possible, then pumping it into the pipeline at a record rate. And she couldn't allow anyone or anything to stop her.

Not even a sun god whose kiss contained fire.

# Two

Tess stumbled out to the terrace clutching a bottle of aspirin in one hand and sunglasses in the other. As soon as the daylight hit her eyes, she groaned and carefully eased on her sunglasses.

"Coffee, ma'am?" Guadalupe asked. Guadalupe was one of four people who worked in and around the house and whose salary was included in the price of the lease.

She started to nod, then immediately realized her mistake as pain jolted through her head. "Yes, please," she whispered.

Gratefully she sank into a chair in front of the table, where breakfast had already been laid out. She took a searing gulp of coffee, downed four aspirin, then slumped back against the chair. Damn gulls. They sounded fiendishly cheerful. And...*loud.* Lord help her, were they that loud every morning?

She'd never had a hangover before, and if she lived through this one, she swore she'd never have one again.

"Is there anything else you'd like, ma'am?"

She almost jumped. She'd forgotten Guadalupe's presence. Warily she eyed the table. Orange juice, fruit, sausage, eggs and an assortment of rolls, jellies and breads— enough to feed your basic small army.

"This will do for now, thank you."

The thing was, her intake of alcohol had always been limited to the occasional beer or a glass of wine with dinner. Even in college, when most kids were celebrating their freedom from their parents with copious amounts of drinking, she'd spent her time sating her appetite for learning about business and oil. Succeeding had always been the most important thing for her, and it still was. She was convinced she could overcome this hangover just as she overcame all obstacles—by sheer determination. If she stayed really still...

*Tess.* Nick paused at the bottom of the terrace steps. She was already at the table, though it didn't look as if she'd eaten anything yet. Her head was resting on the back of the chair, with her loose blond hair hanging down behind it and blowing lightly in the breeze. The hemline of her short, simple blue dress cut across her upper thighs. The morning sun gilded the skin of her bare arms and legs.

How in the hell was he supposed to keep his mind on business when she looked like that?

It was the same problem he'd had last night. Due to his research, he'd thought he was fully prepared for her. But all it had taken was one look and he'd known he wasn't prepared for her.

He hadn't known that one look at her would transfix him. He hadn't anticipated that each time she talked to a friend, her face would light up so entrancingly that it would take his breath away, nor how a fleeting, anxious expression would make him want to be by her side to ward off whatever or whoever was responsible for the look. He hadn't known that when he took her into his arms he would feel a powerful punch in the gut and, lower, a hardening that made him want her to the point of pain.

He'd definitely been thrown off his stride.

Still, he never should have strung her along as he had. He should have told her right up front who he was and what he wanted.

But...her blue eyes had sparkled with such a delightful curiosity as she'd sparred with him that he hadn't been able to resist. And as they'd danced, she'd moved against him with a beguiling, unconscious fluidity that had made him crave her with a strength that had been nearly impossible to ignore.

And her soft, full lips... They'd beckoned him to taste. *Honey.* They'd tasted like honey and whiskey—potent and unforgettable. Still, he never should have kissed her, because with one kiss, he'd known it wouldn't be enough.

Except it *had* to be.

What he wanted from her was far too important for him to let his sexual urges get the best of him. No matter what happened this morning, he had to remember that.

He climbed the steps to the terrace.

"Good morning."

She started at the quiet, deeply masculine voice. Slowly she pushed her sunglasses to the top of her head and squinted up at Nick Trejo. Sunlight radiated around him like a brilliant nimbus. She pulled her sunglasses down to cover her eyes. "Good morning." She straightened.

After last night, she should have known better than to arrange a meeting with him this early *and* outside. She should have known the sun would be more intense wherever he was. But, unwilling to dredge up the memories of *why* she hadn't been thinking straight last night, she decided there was nothing to be done about her decision now. He was here, and she was just going to have to deal with it. With *him*. "Have a seat."

He smiled at her, and she shut her eyes. She'd planned to look not only presentable for their meeting this morning but businesslike. Unfortunately, she'd barely managed to slip on a short cotton shift and sandals. And her hair... Normally she wore it up or secured in some way, but with some heavy metal rock band's percussion section currently booming its merry way through her head, she'd barely been able to run a comb through it.

Opening her eyes and watching as Nick settled himself into the chair across from her, she considered whether or not she could blame him for her hangover. No, she decided. To be fair, she couldn't.

After all, it wasn't his fault that her reaction to him had unnerved her to the point that she'd ordered the bartender to keep her glass filled all night. Besides, she seemed to remember having a really great time.

"Help yourself to anything you like."

"I'll just have coffee." He reached for the carafe, poured himself a cup, then glanced over the terrace and lawn. "You must have had a terrific cleanup crew. If I hadn't been here last night, I wouldn't have known there'd been a party."

"Really?" She didn't bother to conduct her own survey. The movement would have hurt. As he had the night before, Nick was holding all her attention. He was casually dressed in jeans, boots and a rosy beige open-necked shirt beneath a medium brown sport jacket. And his amber eyes were even more vivid in his tanned face than they had been last night.

It didn't matter if it was night or day, she reflected ruefully. It didn't matter if he was dressed up or down. His virile masculinity was enough to stop the heart of a healthy woman. Fortunately for her, she wasn't at all well this morning. She reached for her cup and downed more coffee.

He studied her for several moments. "I gather your party lasted well into the night?"

"I must look even worse than I think I do," she murmured, then watched as his lips curved ever so slightly upward into a half smile.

The sight of his lips brought back the weak, heated way she'd felt when he'd kissed her. Funny. She would have thought the impact of his smile and the sight of his lips would affect her less this morning. After all, everything in her body was hurting, right down to her toenails. Plus she was wearing sunglasses with the added precaution of ultraviolet protection. But...

"Actually, you look quite beautiful. And I like your hair loose."

...he affected her more.

A flush rushed to her face, and self-consciously she raised a hand to her hair. Then she realized what she was doing and dropped her hand. "Thank you." The sooner she got this meeting over with, the better. "Are you sure you don't want anything other than coffee?"

*Food.* That reminded her. If the way her stomach felt was a color, it would be green. For all she knew, she *was* green. Maybe she would feel better if she tried to eat something. One thing was for sure, it couldn't make her feel any worse. At least, she hoped it couldn't.

"I've already had breakfast. The coffee is all I want."

"Okay." She glanced at her watch. A mistake. She

couldn't get the numbers to focus. Then again, he didn't need to know that. "You have fifteen minutes before the world figures out that I'm awake and starts calling and or party stragglers come down in search of breakfast." Cautiously she eyed a wheat roll, then tore a small part of the roll off and carefully ate it. If it stayed down, she would consider herself ahead of the game.

"I realize what an important woman you are, and believe me, I'm very grateful to you for working me into your packed schedule."

He'd said it with a straight face, but a light in his eyes told her that he was mocking her. At any other time she would have called him on it, but not this morning. It would take more effort than she was willing to exert right now. Besides, in the next moment, his expression turned serious.

He leaned back in his chair and fixed his intense amber gaze on her. "There are two things you need to know about me. One, I'm a professor of archaeology at the University of Texas, though currently I'm on sabbatical."

"Archaeology?" Clever cover for a sun god, she thought, and might have laughed at herself if she hadn't been so convinced it would jar loose something in her throbbing head.

She had to get past that sun god analogy, that amazing kiss they'd shared last night and those amber eyes of his that even now were heating her skin. She had to consider him as she would any other business person who was coming to her with a request.

Simple.

She just wished she knew how to do it.

"The other thing you need to know is that in the 1880's my great-grandfather discovered a rich vein of gold in the Sierra Madre mountains in Northern Mexico. It was an enormous find. He literally mined a fortune out of those mountains, and he had great dreams for that gold.'' Nick's voice was strong, and his gaze never once left her face. "He turned it into bullion and loaded it aboard a ship, the *Águila,* at the port of Tampico. The ship's destination was here.'' His index finger pointed to the table, indicating Corpus Christi. "That fortune was to be the start of a new life for him here in Texas. His plan was to buy a vast amount of land, found a great ranch and build an empire.''

The aspirin seemed to be working a little. It had muffled the acute pounding in her head to a dull pounding. She risked another bite of the roll and washed it down with more coffee. "That's very interesting, but what does your family's history have to do with me and my current drilling site?''

"Just listen. Please.''

In many different and unusual ways, the man defined the word power, but he'd said please to her with a sincerity and a supplication she wouldn't have thought him capable of. In that moment she knew she would sit there and listen until he finished his story. "All right.''

"The *Águila* had almost reached its destination when it met a hurricane. It was a killer. At a certain point, it turned away from the land and headed back out to sea. It caught the ship up and blew it farther out into the Gulf. The waves were too high, the ship took on too much water, and it sank.''

She rubbed her aching forehead and wondered how long hangovers lasted. "What a shame, and after he'd worked so hard.''

"The loss of the gold all but killed him. He had what I suppose today we would call a nervous breakdown, but somehow he managed to go back to the Sierra Madre one last time. However, in his absence, other prospectors had descended on the mine, and his heart wasn't in it anymore.

He managed to extract only a meager amount before he left the mountain for good. Back in Texas, he bought a relatively small amount of land outside Uvalde and ran cattle on it until he died.''

''It must have been very hard for him,'' she said, for want of anything better to say. Nick was a compelling man who could affect her with a mere look or touch, and his story was a sad one that moved her. Yet she had a mountain of her own problems waiting for her as soon as she stepped into the house and sat down at her desk, plus she had this damn hangover to deal with.

As if he could sense her mind wandering, Nick eyed her consideringly. ''I don't think you can imagine the full extent of how hard it was for him, because even I can't. I only know that he was a man of great pride and felt humiliated by his failure. To build his self-esteem, he talked incessantly to the people he came to know in and around Uvalde, telling them about the great fortune that he'd wrested from the mountains, then lost. Unfortunately, none of them believed his story of how close he'd come to founding an empire, and they scorned him. He died brokenhearted.''

Through the windows of the house, she could see Ron already handling calls, but she'd committed to hearing Nick out and that was just what she planned to do. ''Your family certainly has an interesting history.''

She'd managed half of the wheat roll, and despite the color and uncertainty of her stomach, she was pleased the roll was staying down. She still didn't have a clue what Nick's story had to do with her, but because of his *please,* she waited.

''History, yes. History that has worked its way down through the generations. I grew up on that history. My grandfather inherited the bill of lading for the gold that had been boarded on that ship.''

"Your great-grandfather had the bill of lading? Then why didn't he simply show it to his neighbors?''

"He did. They thought it was a forgery, but his son, my grandfather, never thought it was, and neither did I.''

Over his shoulder, she saw Ron answering another phone call, and she prayed it wasn't Jimmy Vega with yet another problem. Jimmy was the best tool pusher in the business, and she'd chosen him to supervise the entire operation. In turn, he had put together the best crew of roughnecks there was. Still, everything about this particular operation had been hard so far. They hadn't even been drilling a week, yet time and again, the axiom that what can go wrong will go wrong had been proven true. "Again, Nick, it's all very interesting, but—''

"I've found the shipwreck and the gold.''

Ron came striding onto the terrace, carrying the portable phone, mouthing Jimmy Vega's name. Damn. She really did need to talk with Jimmy. But there was Nick, sitting across from her, and there was no way she would be able to focus on Jimmy as long as Nick's amber eyes were trained so intently on her. She motioned Ron away. A look of surprise crossed his face, but he turned back to the house. "I'm sorry, Nick. What were you saying?''

"I said I've found the gold and I'm ready to start excavating it.''

"Well, congratulations.'' She tried to infuse as much enthusiasm as possible into her congratulations, but she couldn't say it with any strength or volume. Even though the percussion section in her head had quieted, the rest of the band was still playing.

"Congratulations aren't in order yet. I've got a serious problem.''

She exhaled a long breath. "Look, Nick, I could match you problem for problem and more than likely have a stack of problems left over. I've listened to your story, as I said I would, but now I need to get back to work."

"I'm not through."

"I'm sorry, but you are. At least with me." At any other time, she would gladly have lingered over her coffee and listened to Nick. He had the ability to touch and affect her in a way no other man ever had. But there was nothing normal or right about her current circumstances, and there wouldn't be for months to come. She started to push her chair away from the table.

"The *Águila* and the gold are not far from your drilling site, which is why I'm here."

She stilled.

"It's perched atop a scarp. You're drilling in a highly overpressurized zone. It will take only one catastrophe to send the *Águila* sliding off that salt ridge and into the abyss, where it will be buried so deep, it will more than likely be lost forever. Hell, even a series of minor catastrophes would do it."

There was only one thing she could say. "You're right."

He nodded, apparently satisfied that she understood. "I need time to shore up the ship, to brace it in such a way that it will be protected from whatever happens on your rig."

She rubbed her aching forehead, trying to focus. "I don't see how you can really do that."

"It'll be hard, but I can try to make sure it will be safeguarded as much as possible, and then I can pray like hell. Besides, with the crew you've got, plus modern technology, the possibility of a full catastrophe such as a blowout is considerably lessened. But there are other things. There are fault lines down there that would easily channel vibrations

of any sort from your rig over to the *Águila*.'' Pausing, he
looked at her in an assessing way. ''That's why I'm here
to ask you to stop drilling for at least three months.''

''At *least?*'' If she hadn't been sitting, she might have
fallen. As it was, the percussion section of the band in her
head returned. He had no idea what he was asking of her.
''Nick, there's no way I could stop for even a week's
time.''

His body tensed. She didn't see it; she felt it in the air
between them.

''What's the matter, Ms. Baron? Aren't you rich enough
yet?''

The question hit her like a slap. ''No, as a matter of fact
I'm not, Mr. Trejo.''

Nick didn't move, not a muscle, not an eyelash. ''Funny,
you didn't strike me as the greedy type.''

''Do you honestly think you have the right to call me
greedy? You're asking me to give up three valuable months
of an operation that will bring in millions so that you can
have three months to ensure you can safely harvest a crop
of gold worth millions.''

Cold amber eyes stared at her.

Ron walked out again, the phone in his hand, an anxious
expression on his face. ''Vega insists on talking to you.''

She reached for the phone just as Nick rose. ''Hang on
a minute, Jimmy.'' She covered the mouthpiece and looked
at Nick.

''I won't take up any more of your time this morning.''
He glanced at his watch. ''I'll pick you up this evening at
seven.''

''Excuse me?''

He was already walking away from her. ''Seven,'' he
called as he disappeared from the terrace.

Seven? Had he just asked her for a date? A *date?* It was

hard for her to imagine Nick doing something as mundane as asking a woman for a date. He must want more time to try to change her mind, and there was no rule that said she had to go. Still...

"Tess? *Tess?*"

She glanced at the phone, then lifted it to her ear. "Sorry, Jimmy. What's happened now?"

Nick pulled his car onto the road that would take him to the little house he was renting. Tess Baron was every bit as smart and tough as he'd thought she would be. He'd known she wouldn't be an easy sale. Hell, why should she be? What he was asking of her required an enormous sacrifice on her part.

But he'd really thought that on some deep level she would understand and comply. He *still* had hope that she would.

His hand tightened on the steering wheel. Damn it. Why couldn't he just have kept his hands off her last night? Why couldn't he have kept his mind on business? It would have made things between them so much easier.

But now his personal feelings were in the mix, infusing every word, every gesture, with the possibility of volatility. How else could he explain his need to stand up from that table, circle it and pull her into his arms for a long, deep kiss, despite the fact that she'd told him no?

He exhaled a long breath. Obviously he was going to have to get his fast-growing appetite for her under control. He was also going to have to present what he was asking of her in an entirely different way. In effect, he was going to have to set a trap.

He had a little over nine hours to set things in motion, and there would be no margin for error. After this evening, he wouldn't get another chance to change Tess's mind.

Abruptly he took a turn and headed in a different direction.

Six forty-five. It had taken a while, but Tess could now see the face of her watch quite clearly. Nick was supposed to arrive in fifteen minutes, and she had no idea where they were going, or even if this was to be another business meeting or a genuine date.

If Nick planned to spend their time together attempting to convince her to cease her drilling, it would make for a very long and difficult evening for her. But today, as she'd thought about the coming evening, she'd been alarmed to discover that, even if that were his plan, she still wanted to go with him. Which was exactly why she needed to find out up front what he had in mind.

She had all the risk she could handle in her professional life, which was the reason she'd never allowed any risk to enter her personal life. Then last night Nick had appeared, and she hadn't had to look twice to know that, in one way or another, he would be a risk for a woman, a danger for a woman's heart.

Tonight was a prime example. She had no idea where he planned to take her, or why. She only knew she wanted to go. However, she had no intention of allowing that to happen unless he told her it would be a social evening.

She'd chosen an outfit that was suitable for a date. It was a red, sleeveless, A-line knit dress, with a matching cashmere sweater casually tied around the neckline. Her open-toed shoes with a midsize heel were also red. Last but not least, she'd wound her hair into a loose French twist.

If it turned out that Nick planned on talking business, she would politely turn him down, then treat herself to dinner and maybe even a movie. She just wished she knew what he had in mind.

As the day progressed, the pain in her head had lessened and her stomach had calmed. The party guests who stayed over had all left, and the house had quieted. Still, the day hadn't exactly gone great.

There had been all kinds of problems on the rig, from broken drill bits to machinery failure to tangled lines. Sometimes she thought the operation was jinxed—but she couldn't afford to think like that.

If anyone could handle the problems and bring in the oil, it was Jimmy. *If* there was oil to find.

She shook her head, then bent her head to rub her brow. That was something else she couldn't afford to think about. Every one of the tests had looked great, but they were just that—tests. Despite the sophistication of today's testing, in the end, drilling for oil was still very much a wildcatting venture. There were so many variables. To compete in the market, you had to have money, nerves of steel, a large portion of luck, perfect timing and, last but not least, a great instinct for oil.

So far, her wells were bringing in money in amounts that would make anyone deliriously happy. Anyone, that is, except her father.

She glanced at her watch again and noticed that her heart was beating just a little harder as the time drew closer to Nick's arrival. She drew a deep breath of the sea air to compose herself. Tomorrow she was scheduled to fly out to the rig for an inspection, plus an up-to-date cost-and-time report from Jimmy. But for tonight, well, she'd see.

"You look lovely."

She turned, and there he was, all darkness and brilliance, outlined against the sun. Her heart jumped into high gear.

"Thank you. Since I didn't know where we were going, I wasn't certain what to wear." Lord, she sounded like a flustered schoolgirl about to go out on her first date.

His gaze slowly raked her, his lips curved upward. "You chose perfectly."

Which told her exactly nothing. "Then where are we going?"

He held his hand out to her, and before she could stop herself, she took it.

"We're going a place that I love, and by the time we leave, I'm hoping you're going to feel the same way." He began to draw her toward his car, parked at the side of the house.

Abruptly she stopped and pulled her hand from his. "I don't like guessing games, Nick. You and I have been there and done that—last night, as a matter of fact. So what's this all about? Is this going to be a social evening? Or are you going to spend it trying to get me to change my mind about your request? Because if that's the case, you should know right now that it won't work. There's no way I can put off production for three months, and quite frankly, I don't want to spend an evening arguing with you about it."

He stared at her for several moments. Surprisingly his gaze didn't sear as it had the evening before, but rather caressed.

She felt his gaze as a gentle touch all over her body, and as she did, she discovered that gentleness from Nick was a powerful thing. It liquefied her bones. It made her want things for which she had neither the time nor the inclination. Even more remarkable, he wasn't even touching her.

"You've made your position abundantly clear," he said softly. "And as to the question of whether or not this will be a social evening, it's my hope that it will be."

He was saying all the right words, yet she wasn't sure she believed him. Then again, why shouldn't she? To her knowledge, he hadn't lied to her. Last night and this morning, he'd been completely up-front about what he wanted.

She'd told him no, and now he was telling her that he hoped their evening would be a social one. Her hopes matched his exactly.

She couldn't remember the last real date she'd been on, probably because it had been years. And Nick Trejo was the most intriguing man she'd ever met. Chances were their paths wouldn't cross again, yet tonight would be an opportunity for her to spend an interesting evening with an extremely interesting man.

And if his gaze burned or liquefied, and if his touch raised emotions that made her remember for the first time in a long time that she was a woman with normal wants and desires, so be it. Being with him made her forget, if only for a little while, the pressure that was her life.

With a smile, she reached for his hand.


"The airport? Nick, what are we doing at the airport?"

As he steered his car toward one of the outlying hangars, he glanced at her. "I've borrowed a friend's plane to take us to dinner."

Panic rose in her throat, yet there was no real reason. "Look, it's very nice of you to go to all this trouble for our dinner, but it's not necessary."

"I wanted to."

She shook her head, still fighting the mysterious panic. "I've had a rough day, and I'd just as soon stay in town."

He pulled the car into a parking space and switched it off. Turning toward her, he angled his arm along the top of her seat. "This isn't going to require any effort for you, Tess. I promise. All you have to do is sit beside me and relax."

Sit beside him and relax. *That* was the problem. Relaxing while she was sitting beside him in the close confines of a car had turned out to be harder than she had thought it would be. She'd been much too aware of him. She'd found herself mesmerized as she'd watched the confident way his hands had held the wheel and the quick, instinctive way he'd responded to every bump and curve in the road. Around his wrist he wore a slim, stainless steel watch that subtly spoke of masculinity as well as competency.

"If it's your safety you're concerned about, don't be. I'm an excellent pilot. As for the plane, it's the newest in Cessna's fleet and is serviced regularly after every flight. If those two things weren't true, I wouldn't have considered this trip."

"It's not that."

His tone lightened. "Well, it can't be that I'm the first man to ask you to fly to a special place for dinner."

She let out a pent-up breath. "No, you're not the first."

"When you were asked, did you go?"

"Yes."

"Then what's the problem?"

"No problem." She rubbed her forehead. There was no pain, but she felt a growing tension in her scalp, and Nick was the cause. In the short time she'd known him, he'd surprised her, but he hadn't made one move or said one thing to hurt her. Why, then, was her scalp tightening? And why did her instincts tell her to remain on guard? "Mostly I've gone with groups of friends."

"And not one particular man?"

"Once or twice. Look—"

"Please, Tess. This is important to me, and I've already made special arrangements."

Damn it, he'd said *please* again. Plus, she really did want to spend this evening with him. Most likely it would be the only one she'd ever get. Their objectives were so diametrically opposed that she could see no future for them. But for tonight, she really wanted to forget their differences and see if she could find any similarities. If she could find even one, she would consider the evening a success.

"Tess?"

She nodded. "Let's go."

Minutes later, she was buckling herself into the passenger seat beside him. And she couldn't help but notice as they took off that they were flying directly into the sun.

# Three
―――――

**"U**valde? This restaurant that you love so much is in Uvalde, Texas?"

The plane glided to a stop. Then and only then did Nick look at her. "Trust me. You're going to love dinner."

She mentally shrugged. He'd engaged her in pleasant small talk for most of the trip, and she'd actually enjoyed the flight. He had a quick mind that she appreciated, and not once had he mentioned anything about the *Águila* or her drilling.

But as soon as they'd touched down, her original uneasiness had returned. Stupid, really. He certainly hadn't dragged her here, kicking and screaming. She'd wanted to come. Still…

As she came down the stairs of the plane, he offered her a steadying hand. An unnecessary gesture, but definitely a nice one, and after she reached the ground, he continued to hold her hand. "I'm really hoping you'll like what I've planned."

His suddenly serious expression took her aback. "I'm sure I will."

"Good." He stared at her as if he were searching for something in her, or maybe even in himself, but in the end he shook his head.

"Nick? Is there something wrong?"

"Not a thing." He lightly tugged her hand. "Come on. The car is just around the corner."

The car he guided her to was a spotlessly clean, beautifully preserved 1975 Cadillac.

"Is this car a rental?" she asked.

"No. It belongs to my family."

"Your family?"

"My grandparents."

"Oh. So they live in Uvalde?"

"That's right."

Everything was beginning to make sense. "I wondered how a restaurant in Uvalde could have become such a special place to you. You were raised here, right?"

For some reason her remark drew a smile from him, and her heart gave a hard thud. She returned his smile. "Let me guess. This place serves great Tex-Mex, right?"

"On occasion, but not tonight. Hope you're not too disappointed."

She shook her head. "I can get my fill of Tex-Mex in Corpus."

"Good." His smile warmed her inside and out, and she realized that whatever wariness she'd been feeling had disappeared. For the first time since she'd looked across the terrace and seen him, she was totally at ease with him.

He turned onto a highway, then gunned the car so that it zoomed ahead. Given Nick's special affinity with the sun, she wasn't surprised to see that they were still heading west. But given the time of evening, the sun had disappeared, leaving behind only trails of muted reds and oranges on the horizon as a reminder of its existence.

"You said you're a professor at the university?"

"That's right."

"So then you have a home in Austin?"

"Yes. Do you know Austin?"

"I went to school there. It was a requirement for me and my two sisters."

"Requirement?"

She smiled dryly. "Oh, yeah. It had to be the University of Texas or it would be nothing."

"Sounds as if your father had very definite ideas."

"That's one way of putting it." Dictatorial was another.

"One thing about it—no one can make a mistake by going there. What was your degree in?"

"Petroleum engineering." Such a shame, she thought. She'd never had a professor who looked even remotely like Nick. She could only imagine the clamor of the young, attractive women lining up, trying to get into his classes. In fact, if he'd been a professor there when she'd attended, she would have been clamoring right along with the others. She smiled to herself at the thought. "Austin's a really great city."

"It's also a wonderful place to live and relatively easygoing."

"Not like Dallas, huh?"

His head swung around. "You don't like living in Dallas?"

Even she had heard the wistfulness in her voice, so she wasn't surprised that he had. "Oh, I love it. There's always something happening there, and it's a great base for international dealings." It was the truth. Only the word *easy-*

*going* had caused her wistfulness, though she wasn't sure why. Her life was made up of discipline, drive and ambition. She'd never known any other way.

"In this day and time of faxes and modems, I imagine you could work anywhere and still maintain international ties without any problems."

"I'm not sure that's entirely true. For the type of business I do, it's almost imperative to have an international airport close by, and Dallas does."

He turned off the highway onto a two-lane country road. "DFW is a short flight away from Austin."

"Uh-huh." His Chamber of Commerce-like promotion of Austin was interesting, but it didn't affect her one way or another. Her home was in Dallas because her uncle and her father had decided the offices of Baron International should be there. And as soon as she'd graduated from college at the age of twenty, she'd dived headfirst into the deep end of the high-tech, high-stress world of the oil business. She loved it. She thrived on it. She was good at it. She'd never minded the long hours or the pressure of risking huge amounts of money on what, in the end, came down to her instincts.

Only her father's ability to reach beyond the grave and affect her life, along with those of her sisters, had sucked the fun out of her work. And the last couple of years, that same ability had accelerated her stress to warp speed.

Suddenly she glanced around her, gazed out the back window, then looked at Nick. "I may have my directions wrong, but isn't town that way?" She pointed a window to the east.

He eased his foot off the gas pedal. "Yes, but our dinner is this way."

"Oh." Once again she looked around her. "But this is all country. There's nothing out here."

"Not quite nothing." They topped a hill, then Nick took a left onto a dirt road. "We're almost there."

She sat back and watched as the road unfolded before her—around a bend, along a line of broken fence, up a slight hill with buffalo grass growing on either side. Then ahead a house gradually appeared, starkly outlined against the dusky sky.

The house was two stories, with gingerbread trim that outlined its porch. Cream-colored paint peeled off its wooden exterior. Two chimneys, one at either end of the house jutted out of the shingled roof. A weather vane perched between the chimneys, along with several lightning rods. It looked abandoned. "This isn't where we're going to eat dinner, is it?"

"Yes." He pulled the car to a stop in front of the house, then got out, walked around to open her door and offered his hand.

She took it and slid out. There wasn't another car in sight, nor could she see any lights in the house. "But it doesn't look as if there's anyone here but us."

"There's not. This is going to be a very exclusive dinner."

"But—"

With one of his slight smiles that made her skin tingle, he lightly squeezed her hand. "Come on. This has always been my favorite place to eat, and I'm anxious to share it with you."

"Ooo-kay." No sense backing out now. She'd known that an evening with Nick would be out of the ordinary. She just hadn't known *how* out of the ordinary.

She climbed the front steps, looking around her as she went. Then Nick pushed open the unlocked front door, and she walked into a darkened hall. Almost immediately, a heavenly smell wafted toward her.

He flipped on a light switch. Completely mystified, she saw faded wallpaper and a scarred wooden floor.

"Whatever that smell is, it's *wonderful*."

For the first time he fully smiled at her. "I can assure you that the food will be as wonderful as it smells. Would you like to wash up?"

"Yes, thank you."

He pointed toward another hall at a right angle to the one they were in. "First door on your right." He pointed down the main hallway to an open doorway. "Come in there when you're finished."

"If that's where the heavenly smells are originating from, I'll be right in."

She found the bathroom and shut the door after her. Out-of-date fixtures greeted her, along with towels and wash-cloths that, though faded, looked freshly washed. The wallpaper was peeling in spots. The linoleum had holes worn into it, yet the smell of a recently used lemon-scented cleaner hung in the air.

She shook her head in wonder. This place certainly wasn't a restaurant, yet the smells coming out of the kitchen were making her salivate. She'd never once entertained the notion that there was anything simple about Nick. Now, she realized, she was about to learn just how complicated he was.

And if in the end she discovered that he'd planned this evening as a way to convince her to stop her drilling, she wouldn't be surprised. But she *would* be deeply, deeply disappointed.

Damn the man, anyway. Why hadn't he just taken Ron's no for an answer when Ron had told him he couldn't see her? Why did he have to crash her birthday party and bring more complications into her life at a time when she could barely handle the ones she already had?

She sighed. Because he was Nick Trejo, that was why.

Minutes later, she walked into a dimly lit kitchen. Small lamps were lit at either end of an aged sideboard. A square table graced the middle of the room. Covered by a blue tablecloth, set for two with blue and white plates and lit by a short, round blue candle whose base was surrounded by field daises, the table looked as if it had just come off the pages of *Country Homes*. In fact, the whole kitchen did.

On the counter, a freshly baked loaf of bread rested on a cutting board with a bottle of wine beside it. Beef stew simmered in a large pot on the stove. Nick stood at the table, forking a crisp salad into two small bowls that matched the plates.

She eyed him wryly. "This is a set, isn't it? And everything here is a prop, right?" But even as she said it, she knew she was wrong. Whatever was happening, she hadn't figured it out yet.

"A set?" He took the salad bowl to the counter. "You mean like for a TV show?"

She shook her head. "Never mind."

"Take a seat and I'll pour you some wine."

She settled into one of the chairs and watched him as he poured the wine into two glasses, then carried the glasses to the table. He'd taken off his jacket and rolled up his sleeves, and she was suddenly struck by how comfortable and at home he seemed.

"Okay, Nick, I think now is a good time to tell me what exactly is going on. No one lives in this house, do they?"

"In one way, yes, but in another way, no."

"I'm not interested in playing guessing games, Nick. Exactly whose house is this?"

"My grandparents'. They live in town now."

"So no one lives here."

"They live here, too."

"But you just said..." She waved her hand in front of her as if she were erasing her words. "Forget it. Let me try another question. Where did the food come from?"

"My sister, Kathie." He brought the bread to the table and sliced off several pieces, then angled the knife he'd used across the cutting board. "She's married to a pharmacist, and they live in town with their two daughters. But my grandmother taught her to cook, and everything we're going to eat tonight is from my grandmother's recipe file. Believe me, our dinner is guaranteed to be delicious."

She only had to inhale to know he was right. She sipped her wine as she tried to understand the rest of what he'd said. "So let me get this straight. Your sister came out here, cooked all this and then left right before we arrived?"

Deftly he ladled stew into two bowls. "She knew our schedule, so it was fairly easy for her to have everything ready, and she didn't mind at all."

"That's very nice of her. She must have done this same sort of thing for you before."

He paused and looked at her. "No."

"You mean you've never brought other women out here to this same sort of setup?"

"No, I haven't."

"Really." Disbelief flattened her tone.

He left his task and moved to her, his broad-shouldered, leanly muscled frame radiating a barely contained electric tension that seemed, with his next breath, to have the potential to turn to danger.

How could she have forgotten that when she'd first seen him last night, her instincts had told her he was a man who should be treated with caution? With her next breath came the answer. Obviously his kiss the evening before had knocked all sense from her head. Then, this evening, he'd been a charming host, lulling her into a false sense of security. But still, she should have remembered.

He braced his hands on the table and leaned toward her, his amber eyes bright against his dark skin. "This is the very first time I've ever asked Kathie to do something like this, and when I told her who my guest would be, she was more than willing to cook our dinner."

"You told her who I was." The light dawned. "I see. So it all comes back to my drilling site, doesn't it?"

He lapsed into silence as he returned to the stove for the two bowls of stew. He took his time, making sure everything was on the table that needed to be. Was he trying to think of an answer she might find acceptable? Or was he simply going to ignore her question?

"There was no need for this elaborate ruse, Nick." Her tone held deliberate and cutting derision. "I could have told you no back home as well as I can tell you no here. As a matter of fact, I did."

He settled into the chair across from her and leveled a piercing gaze on her. "I won't lie to you, Tess. Part of this trip does involve me trying to get you to change your mind and stop your drilling for three months."

"Then you haven't been *listening* to me. I've already told you—"

He held up his hand. "But at the same time, I meant it when I said that I hoped this evening would be a social one." Without dropping his gaze from her, he ran his fingers up and down the stem of his wineglass. "The truth is, Tess, I want to get to know you better."

His amber eyes glittered like stars in a dark, stormy night sky. If there was some way to look at his face without having to see his eyes, she reflected wryly, she would be a lot better off.

"You see," he said quite casually, "I want you. I have since the first moment I laid eyes on you."

The breath caught in her throat. "You—"

"I want you much more than I know how to tell you." He paused, his gaze never leaving hers. "I didn't count on that happening. Last night, when I went to your party, I went strictly for business reasons. But then I saw you, and felt you against me as we danced—" his gaze dropped to her lips "—and I kissed you. And I left wanting much more."

She tried to swallow but found her throat constricted. She took a gulp of wine, tried to swallow again and this time was successful. "You are either very direct or you're lying for your own ends."

"I wouldn't lie to you, Tess. Not about this."

"And how am I supposed to know that?" She heard the hint of desperation in her voice, but there was nothing she could do about it. "I just met you last night. Then tonight, under the guise of having dinner, you flew me out here to this isolated house."

"We *are* about to have dinner, so that was no lie. And I'm not lying to you about wanting you. Deep down, you must know that."

She did know it, which was why she was feeling so desperate. He'd declared desire, not love, which was good. She wouldn't have believed him if he'd said he loved her. But either way, he was bringing emotions into their relationship that she wasn't prepared to deal with. In reality, she simply didn't know how.

"I hope you feel the same way I do."

Damn. That was one of the problems. She did. But she'd never been any good at this sort of thing. It was why she had friends instead of lovers. Give her a tough negotiation to handle, or a complicated drilling site to tackle, and she was in her element. But Nick, with his commanding presence and his heated stare, threw her. She had no practice with womanly wiles.

Her sister Jill would know exactly how to handle Nick. Jill was an expert at luring men into her sophisticated web, then, more often than not, she would walk away and leave them hanging. Even Kit would know. Kit would simply give a toss of her red hair and laugh, and within minutes she would have a man wrapped around her little finger. Then she, too, would walk away.

But Tess didn't know how to play games with men. All she knew how to do was to tell the truth, and in this case, she really, really didn't want to do that. The truth would make her vulnerable, something she couldn't afford to be with this man. The truth would also make it almost impossible for her to walk away, even though that was exactly what she would have to do.

"Do you, Tess? Do you want me even a fraction as much as I want you?"

She turned her face away and briefly closed her eyes. She could lie to him, but she was so terrible at it, he would know. There was really only one thing she could tell him. "I wouldn't be here if I didn't."

It was as if a two-ton elephant had just lumbered into the room and sat down at the table with them. They couldn't ignore it. They couldn't make it disappear. It was there, and now they were going to have to figure out what to do with it.

"There's one last thing you should know, Tess, because in some ways it takes us beyond the realm of the feelings that are between the two of us. There are things I hope you will learn while we're here."

"Things?" Her wariness was back, and she didn't even attempt to hide it.

"Things about my family."

She didn't want to do this. She wanted to snap her fingers and be back at the house in Corpus Christi. Alone. And with another snap of her fingers she wanted to make Nick disappear from her life. He came with too many demands, too many complications. But as hard as she'd studied in school, she'd never learned to snap her fingers and make things happen. "Isn't learning about your family the same thing as learning about you?"

"In some ways, I suppose so."

She didn't understand why he would try to separate the two. She didn't even want to understand. She rubbed her brow. "Whether we like it or not, our family dynamics play a huge part in shaping who we are."

His slow smile was warm. "I'm glad you understand that."

She understood it more than he knew. Her own family dynamics were worthy of the fictional Ewings of *Dallas*.

She needed time to regain her balance, so she began to eat the stew, which turned out to be mouthwatering, and was extremely grateful when Nick did the same. For now she was more than happy to pretend she didn't see the elephant.

She knew she was awkward when it came to relationships with men. And when it came to Nick, her awkwardness was multiplied by a thousand. Given the same chance she had, any other woman on the planet would already have cleared the dishes with one sweep of her arm and started making love to Nick right atop his grandmother's kitchen table.

But she couldn't—*wouldn't* do such a thing. She wasn't up to delving any deeper into their mutually declared desire. Not now, with him so close.

At this point, all she wanted was to get home. In the

solitude and safety of her bedroom, she hoped she could get a better perspective on everything that had happened and been said this evening. Because when she faced the desire they felt for each other, she would also have to face the fact that at least part of Nick's desire for her involved what he wanted from her. And that would be extremely hard on her.

Realistically, she knew there were different kinds of seduction, and two kinds were involved here. There was seduction for the purpose of getting someone to have sex with you. And there was seduction for the purpose of getting someone to agree with you.

Nick wanted both, and she didn't think she could handle letting him have either. She didn't have enough experience to be able to tell one type of seduction from the other, so, knowing her, she would concentrate on the desire he made her feel, which from her side would be pure. And in the end, when he walked away from her because she couldn't give him what he wanted, she would be hurt. Badly.

So she deliberately led the conversation down the most innocuous paths she could think of. They talked about the food and she coaxed Nick into telling her anecdotes about his nieces.

She badly needed the time their dinner gave her. The evening wasn't close to being over, yet it had already turned out to be one stunning surprise after another. She needed to catch her breath so she could be ready for the next surprise. Because if there was one thing she was learning, it was that, with Nick, there would be a next surprise.

And that elephant was still sitting there, waiting for them to resolve, one way or another, the issue of their desire for one another.

\* \* \*

Nick cleared the dinner dishes from the table, while Tess lingered over her coffee and a bowl of peach cobbler. "Please remember to tell your sister how much I've enjoyed the dinner."

"I will. She's accustomed to getting compliments on her cooking, but it still makes her day when she receives another."

She took her last bite of cobbler, then pushed the bowl away. In keeping with her plan of maintaining a stream of conversation until they could leave, she asked, "So, tell me about this house. If your grandparents live in town, why is it still fully furnished?"

After he'd stacked the dishes in the sink and squirted them with soap, he turned on the water. "My grandfather has a severe heart problem that needs to be closely monitored. My grandmother's health is better, though at her age, anything could happen. They needed to be in town so they could be closer to their doctor and the hospital. They knew it as well as Kathie and I did."

The water rose higher and higher in the sink until it covered the dishes, then he turned it off. "Still, when it came to the move, they dug in their heels. The only way they would agree was for Kathie and me to promise that this house would still be here for them, just as it always has been. We keep all the utilities on and have the place cleaned once a month. And every once in a while, they drive out here and have lunch and stay an hour or two. It makes them happy and, at the same time, they're safe, which are the two things that count the most." He turned and leaned against the counter.

She smiled. "You know what I think?"

"What?"

"I think they're very lucky to have you and your sister as grandchildren."

"Kathie and I are the lucky ones. They raised us."

She blinked. "How did that come about?"

"Our parents were killed in an airplane crash."

"How awful."

He nodded. "Yes. I was eight, and Kathie was seven. But our grandparents were there for us, so now it's our turn to be there for them."

"That's wonderful," she said seriously.

"What we're doing for them is very little compared to what they did for us."

Damn the man. She couldn't find a thing she didn't like about him. Nevertheless, a single fact remained true. They had opposing interests. She couldn't agree to the postponement of her drilling schedule, and as soon as he realized she couldn't be swayed, she would never see him again.

"You know what I find remarkable? The fact that your parents were killed in an airplane crash, yet here you are, a pilot."

He grinned, and she was momentarily stunned. It was the first time he'd grinned at her, and she was charmed by the hint of the boy behind the man.

"I'm a pilot *because* my parents died in a crash. The crash gave me a strong fear of flying. The only way I could overcome it was to learn all I could about planes and flying."

"And that's the reason you made a point of assuring me how safe our flight would be."

He shrugged. "I worked and studied until I felt that I was the very best pilot I could be. And I won't fly a plane unless I can see its service record and then go over the plane myself. I believe in stacking the odds in my favor."

*He believed in stacking the odds in his favor.* From what she knew of him, his statement made perfect sense, and she wasn't thinking about the way he'd overcome his fear of flying. She pushed herself up from the table and carried the cobbler bowl and her coffee cup to the counter.

"Is that the reason you brought me out here? Do you think that bringing me to your grandparents' house and feeding me your sister's cooking will somehow stack the odds in your favor and I'll just give in?"

"It's part of the reason, but I've already told you that."

For a while during dinner, as she'd listened to him talking about his nieces, she'd done her best to push from her mind his ultimate objective and had tentatively tested the waters of what it was like simply to be a woman on a date with a man to whom she was strongly attracted.

But the harder she'd tried, the harder she'd hit that wall of knowledge that nothing serious could ever develop between them. And instinctively she knew that, emotionally, she would never be able to handle a casual affair, not with any man, but especially not with Nick.

Nick wanted her and would probably be more than satisfied with a casual affair, but she would bet her last dime that, if given the choice, he would forget the affair and choose to have her halt her drilling.

"I can't stop the drilling, Nick. That answer will never change, no matter what you do or say. And I'd like to fly back to Corpus as soon as possible, so let me help you with these dishes. The sooner we get everything put away, the sooner we can leave. Switch places with me. Since you know where things go, I'll wash and you dry." She stepped around him to the sink and plunged her hands into the water.

Watching her, he picked up a dishcloth. "Why are you so anxious to leave? Didn't the dinner live up to my billing?"

"Absolutely. The food was delicious, and the place was

unique.'' She flashed a quick smile at him. ''Thank you for inviting me.''

''You're welcome. But you didn't tell me why you're so anxious to leave.''

''I have a busy day tomorrow, and I need to do some preparatory work tonight before I go to sleep.'' She handed him a plate to dry.

''You keep a grueling schedule. Haven't you ever wanted to just take off somewhere for a day or two?''

''Only occasionally. The reality is I love my work.'' She rinsed off another plate and handed it to him.

Drying the plate, he glanced at her. He couldn't begin to guess what she was thinking, but one thing he knew. She was anxious to leave because she was anxious to get away from him, and under the circumstances, her attitude wasn't entirely unexpected. ''As dates go, I suppose ours hasn't been a huge success.''

''I wouldn't exactly say that. The whole evening has been a very unique experience.''

''Good. I'm glad you think that, because I'd like you to meet my grandparents.''

She handed him a wineglass to dry, with another one quickly following. ''I'd like that, too. Perhaps another time.''

Her answer was automatic, her tone vague. Obviously her mind was already back in Corpus and on what she needed to do there.

God, how he wished the two of them really were on an uncomplicated, getting-to-know-you first date. But more importantly, he would give practically everything he owned if he didn't have to carry through with his plan to snare her in the trap he'd conceived.

Women had come and gone in his life. Sometimes the woman would decide to leave; other times it was his decision. It had never bothered him that he hadn't found the one who would make him forget all others. He was like Tess—his work was all-encompassing to him. His life ranged from the interesting, challenging world of academics to the risky, exciting business of diving for treasure.

But now he'd met Tess, and it had been evident to him from the first that she was different from every other woman he had ever met. And he wasn't only talking about his attraction to her, though there was certainly that. Standing as close to her as he was, he only had to breathe to smell the perfume of her skin. He only had to look over to see how her ivory skin gleamed in the dim lamplight and the way her breasts curved enticingly beneath the red dress. He hadn't yet held her breasts, hadn't yet drawn her nipples into his mouth. And the fact was, he probably never would.

He threw the kitchen towel onto the counter, grabbed her upper arms and pulled her against him. A quiver ran through her body; he felt it beneath his hands as his mouth came down on hers and his tongue plunged deep into her mouth. Heat surged to his loins, and instantly he was hard.

Her wet hands fluttered in the air, then settled on his shoulders. She was giving in to his kiss, accepting it. But more than that, she *wanted* his kiss. He could feel it in the way her body had instantly softened against his, in the urgent way she wound her arms around his neck and clung to him.

Their sudden, mutual need for each other had seemingly sprang from nowhere, but that meant it had been running beneath their skin and through their blood all along.

The knowledge gave him a savage gratification unlike anything he'd ever felt before. She wanted him, and God knew, he wanted her. But if he took her before she agreed to what he wanted... Damn it, he didn't care. He wanted her *now*.

He slid his hands along either side of her jaw, then pressed his lips harder against hers, and she responded by opening her mouth wider. He tilted her head back, then, with a rough sound, once again took deep and full possession of her mouth. Their tongues tangled in a sweet, compelling dance that increased his need with a force that nearly knocked him off his feet.

She tasted of coffee, peaches and honey. No doubt now what she tasted like. The honey had to be her natural taste. And the feel of her—the soft curves of her breast and the smooth skin of her throat—he was fast reaching the point where he was going to have to have her or die from the wanting, so fast that he was nearly dizzy with the need. It was in his bone marrow; it was in his blood.

She moaned, the sound of her satisfaction going deep into his mouth. He swallowed the sound and experienced the combined tastes of her passion and his own. That was it. He'd reached the end of his control. He had to have her. He reached behind her for the zipper of her dress.

Suddenly she pushed herself away from him, catching him so off guard that he had to throw his hand out to grip the counter to steady himself.

"Please...please take me home now." She turned away from him and kept her eyes downcast, as if she couldn't meet his gaze.

He struggled to regain control of his feelings, but it was well-nigh damned impossible. Another minute of her kisses and he would have had her on the kitchen floor, making love to her. Afterward he wouldn't have been sorry, but it wasn't his reaction he would have been concerned about.

"What just happened, Tess?" He asked the question even though he was afraid he knew the answer.

He didn't think for a minute that if they made love, she would change her mind and give him the time he needed.

But *she* might. No matter how many times he could tell her otherwise, she might still think his ultimate purpose in making love to her was to get her to agree to give him the three months he needed to secure the ship and the gold. She would be wrong, but after they'd made love, it wouldn't matter. He would never be able to convince her otherwise, and the damage would be done.

This time he'd almost let his desire overrule his good sense. Damn it, he was still suffering from the lapse. He felt pain in every part of his body. He couldn't afford to lose control like that again. From now on, he had to keep his mind trained on his goal.

Silently he cursed. Logic told him that he should be grateful she had put a halt to what had nearly been fast, hot, hard sex. Even now, powerful feelings were urging him to pull her into his arms and kiss her until they were both mindless with desire and tearing each other's clothes off.

"Nick? I said I'd like to go home now."

He let out a long, shaky breath. "Is that all you've got to say? Don't you think we should talk about what just happened?"

Slowly she turned to face him, her arms wrapped around herself, her face pale. "I don't think there's too much to say about it, except that it shouldn't have happened and we both know why. Now, *please,* I'd like to go home as soon as possible."

This was the moment he'd been dreading since he'd picked her up at her house earlier this evening, the moment that would positively rule out any chance of personal involvement between the two of them ever. "I'm sorry, Tess, but I'm not taking you home tonight."

# Four

"Excuse me? What did you just say?"

He folded his arms across his chest and leaned against the counter. He still needed its stability. "We're going to spend the night here so that in the morning we can drive into town and you can meet my grandparents."

"Tell me you're kidding."

"I'm not kidding."

"I don't have a clue what you think you're doing, Nick, but one way or another, I'm going back home tonight."

He appeared unmoved. "You're the head of Baron's oil division. That means you can take time off whenever you like. What's the problem?"

"The problem is, now is *not* a time I like. In fact, I don't like it even a little bit. You've been told more than once that my schedule is packed. *Believe* it."

He nodded. "Oh, I do. But one more day is not going to make any difference."

Her anger erupted, and her voice rose to a volume few had ever heard from her, though she wasn't screaming. Not yet. "How in the hell do you know that? And just who do you think you are to make this kind of decision for me?" She punched her finger against his chest. "I'll tell you who you are. You're just someone who crashed my party last night. I haven't even known you twenty-four hours, and you think I'm going to let you rule my life? No way!"

"It's very important to me for you to meet my grandparents, so we'll be staying here for the night."

His tone was calm, his expression composed, and she wanted to kill him. "Like hell we will. You can do what you want, but I'm going home."

"You can't."

"Watch me." She wanted to scream and was determined not to, but she couldn't stop her voice from shaking. "I'll simply charter another plane and fly home."

"There is no charter service available here."

"But there are private planes at the airport. I saw them when we flew in. When I get to the airport, I'll simply ask for the name of one of the owners, call him or her up, and charter their plane."

"It's late. Here, people go to bed early because they get up early. They're not going to want to climb out of bed to fly some stranger to Corpus Christi."

"How do you know what they'll want to do? Contrary to what you obviously think, you can't tell what people will or won't do, and you sure as hell can't keep me here against my will."

Still perfectly composed, he shrugged. "Even if you can get someone to agree, which I doubt, how are you going to get to the airport? I'm not taking you."

"I'll call a cab."

"No cab will come this far out, especially this late."

"For enough money—"

He shook his head. "I hate to disillusion you, Tess, but you just may be in the one place on earth where your money won't help you."

"This is unconscionable."

"You're absolutely right. It's also desperation. I want you to meet my grandparents so that you'll understand why the *Águila* and its contents are so important to me."

"And by holding me here against my will, you honestly think that I'll view your request more favorably?"

"It's my only shot, and I've got to take it."

"I've got a news flash for you, Nick. Holding me here will flat out guarantee you won't get even the smallest thing that you want from me."

She thought she saw darkness flash in the depth of his eyes, but he blinked, and then it was gone.

"Like I said, I have to try."

"And so do I." She glanced around the kitchen. "Where's the phone and a phone book? And don't tell me you don't have one. You'd have to have a phone out here in case one of your grandparents got sick while they were visiting."

Silently he pointed to the side of a cabinet where the phone hung. Then he opened a drawer, pulled out the phone book, and handed it to her.

For the next fifteen minutes she called everyone she thought could help her, from cab companies to the airport. She even called the police department, but once they heard her name and who was holding her against her will, they turned less than helpful. As a last-ditch effort, she tried to hire an ambulance, but when she had to admit she wasn't ill, they refused. Finally she tried to get in touch with Ron, but she ended up having to leave a message on the answering machine in his office. She glanced at her watch.

He was probably still out with that new girlfriend he'd met since they'd been in Corpus. It would be just her bad luck if he decided to spend the night at the woman's apartment.

"Not home?" he asked when she hung up.

She sat down at the table and shot him a killing look. "You heard."

While she'd been making her calls, he'd finished cleaning the kitchen, and now he hung the dish towel on a hook. "Frankly, I'm surprised your assistant has a life outside work. I would have figured you'd have him at his desk twenty-four hours a day."

Drumming her fingers on the table, she glanced sightlessly around the room. It wouldn't do her any good to call one or both of her sisters. Instead of offering help, they would laugh themselves silly at the situation she'd gotten herself into.

Nick's deep voice broke into her thoughts. "If you're looking for something to throw at me, please don't go for anything that could break. My grandmother would be very upset."

She glared at him. "And tell me again why I should care? She should have taught you better manners than to kidnap someone."

"May I remind you that you came of your own free will?"

"Because you lied to me."

"I didn't lie to you. I simply didn't tell you the whole truth."

"A lie of omission is still a lie, and you know it."

"I couldn't have gotten you on the plane any other way."

"Oh, sure you could." Her tone was laced with sarcasm. "You had any number of alternatives at your disposal. You could have drugged me, or hit me and knocked me out cold.''

He frowned. ''Do you honestly think I would physically harm you?''

She spread her hands. ''How would I know? I would never have thought you'd kidnap me and keep me here against my will, but I was wrong, wasn't I? You're just full of surprises.'' She began to pace around the kitchen. She always paced when she was agitated and needed to think.

She couldn't call Uncle William for help, because she wouldn't want him upset. And she had no idea how to get hold of Des. His office would know, but his office was closed. As for his home phone, she'd called it so few times that it wasn't a number she had committed to memory, and she knew it would be unlisted. Colin Wynne would come to get her if she called, but she really didn't want her friends to know how easily Nick had duped her.

''Come on, Tess. Don't make such a big deal out of this. We had a nice trip out here, and by your own admission, the dinner was wonderful. Now all I'm asking is that you spend the night in a perfectly nice bedroom with clean sheets on the bed, and I'll have you back in Corpus by lunchtime tomorrow.''

She whirled on him. ''Oh, *that* was good. Just the right touch of sincerity and with a dash of entreaty. And don't forget the kiss. That kiss was quite something. But it was just another weapon in your arsenal, wasn't it? Much like that damn *please* of yours.''

His brow furrowed. ''My please? What are you talking about?''

''Nothing. Absolutely nothing.'' She folded her hands. ''Okay, Nick, I'm going to ask you once again. Will you please take me home?''

He stared at her. Her face was flushed with color. The

pulse at the base of her neck was pounding. He wanted nothing more than to scoop her into his arms, take her into his bedroom, strip her naked and make love to her until they were both satiated. But that was no longer an option. And if he were honest with himself, it never had been.

"I'll show you to your room. It was my sister's room, and there are still a few things of hers left. She laid out something for you to sleep in, plus she left fresh towels and a new toothbrush and toothpaste for you. They're in the bathroom."

"How very kind of her. And thoughtful, definitely thoughtful. You know, I didn't think about it before, but it's obvious now that your sister is in on this crime with you."

"Crime?"

"Quite obviously you're going to find this hard to believe, Nick, but holding someone against their will is a crime. I tried to explain that to the chief of police of this fine town, but he seemed more amused than concerned."

"Uh, yeah. He and I went to school together. And, anticipating how you might react to, uh, staying the night, I gave him a call earlier today and explained the situation."

"Perfect. Just perfect." Her words were cold and sharp as an ice pick.

He levered himself away from the counter and started toward the hall. "Follow me and I'll show you to your room. And if you can't find what you need, just ask."

Tess couldn't sleep.

She was too angry at Nick. He'd quieted her unease at the idea of flying out of Corpus for the evening by telling her he'd made special arrangements for this evening, and she couldn't fault him there. He'd definitely made special arrangements.

But she was just as angry at herself. She should have paid more attention to her initial panic when he'd told her they were going to fly to some undisclosed place for dinner. How could she have been so stupid and naive? She'd trusted him, and he'd betrayed her.

Pulling the pillow over her face, she groaned. Truthfully, trust had only been a small part of the reason she'd gotten on that plane with him. Her attraction to him had been the main reason. She threw the pillow across the room.

Thinking about it, she decided the word *attraction* was way too mild to describe what he made her feel. He hadn't needed knockout drugs or violence to get her on the plane. He'd simply smiled at her and said please and charmed her right into the seat beside his.

But as angry as she was, at him and at herself, it wasn't enough to keep her awake. She was also worried. Bringing in this well on schedule was so vitally important to her that she often spent sleepless nights worrying.

True, it was too early to expect to see oil, but still, she couldn't stop worrying. She was so afraid that somewhere along the line she'd miscalculated, and either they wouldn't strike oil, or they would strike oil but the well wouldn't come in as big as her instincts were telling her it would.

It wasn't an overstatement to say that a major portion of her life would be lost if either of those things happened.

She rolled onto her side. The house was quiet and still. No doubt Nick had fallen asleep with no problem at all. But then, what did he have to worry about? With a stratagem worthy of a battlefield general, he had maneuvered her into a trap and now had her exactly where he wanted her.

Angrily she kicked the covers aside and got out of bed. Nick's sister had left a soft cotton nightshirt on the bed for her to sleep in. It covered her nearly to her knees, and since

Nick was asleep and she had no wish to dig through some-one else's closet, she decided she didn't need a robe.

As quietly as possible, she wandered out of the bedroom, down the hall and into what she presumed was the living room. Carefully, trying not to make a sound, she closed the door. Then, feeling her way around, she turned on the first lamp she came to.

An overstuffed sofa and two comfortable-looking reclin-ers met her gaze. A padded rocker and a table were posi-tioned by a window. Outdated magazines lay on a wooden coffee table. Crocheted doilies covered the arms of the sofa and chairs. A crocheted afghan in green, orange and gold lay over the back of the couch, the hues telling her the afghan had been made some time in the sixties or seventies.

And then there were the pictures, many of them, on the tables, on the mantel and on the walls.

She started with the wall closest to her and worked her-way around the room, turning lamps on and off as she went. A picture of a young bride and groom in sepia tones caught her attention. From the age of the picture and the style of the clothes, she realized it was probably a picture of Nick's grandparents on their wedding day. The young man in the picture looked as if he were about to burst with pride. The young woman's face was full of joy.

Farther on, Tess found another picture of the young woman, only this time she held a baby boy in her arms. The baby had to be Nick's father. As the years passed in pictures, she saw the baby grow into a young man, go off to war and return. His marriage to a lovely young woman was celebrated on another wall. Next, the picture of another baby boy appeared—Nick, she guessed—and, soon after, another baby, a girl, Kathie.

There were no more pictures of Nick's parents, but on another wall she found yearly school pictures of both Nick and Kathie. A smile touched her lips as she went from picture to picture, witnessing Nick turn into the man he was when he graduated from college.

At his college graduation, his proud grandparents stood on either side of him. Kathie must have been taking the picture, she reflected, studying it. Since that picture, Nick had filled out; the lines of his face and body had matured, hardened. But on the day of his graduation, his amber eyes were filled with nothing but happiness and dreams.

She lingered over that picture the longest, wondering about the years between his graduation and now. Since she'd met him, she'd seen him express many emotions, but none of them had been the pure happiness that had been on his face the day of his graduation. As for his dreams, she supposed excavating the *Águila* was his dream. Had that also been his dream back then? Did he have other dreams? And, if so, what were they?

There were other pictures, of course—Kathie's wedding, her two darling little girls, growing up in each succeeding photo.

Now she understood why Nick's grandparents wouldn't let go of this house. Their entire life was right here in this room.

"A lot of pictures, right?"

She stilled, then slowly turned to face Nick. One look at him jolted her to the present. He was wearing only a pair of faded jeans. Everything else—his broad chest, his sinewy arms, his flat abdomen—was bare.

And his jeans left very little to the imagination. The soft-looking denim closely followed the muscled length of his hips, thighs and calves and intimately cupped the large bulge at his crotch.

The sight made her mouth go dry. "Pictures? Yes, there are quite a few."

As he leisurely made his way toward her, shadows from the lamp's light shifted over his face and body, creating mysterious markings and contouring. She should turn her back to him and return her focus to the pictures she'd been studying. That was exactly what she should do. But she couldn't.

As was his way, Nick held her complete attention.

"Kathie and I offered to take down all the pictures and put them up in their new home, but they wouldn't hear of it."

He reached her side, and she could smell soap and heated bare skin. He was too close. She should move, but the intensity of his gaze, such a contrast to the gentleness of his voice, held her where she was.

"My grandmother said if we took the pictures down, they would leave faded spots on the wall. We offered to put up new wallpaper, but they said no. They love this wallpaper. They put it up after my dad came home from the war, and they don't want it taken down. They said the pictures belong in this room, on this wallpaper."

A sleep shirt and a pair of panties didn't constitute a lot of clothes, but at least she was more covered than he was. Why, then, did she feel practically naked? "I think they're right."

In the quiet and darkness of the house, they were both speaking softly, as if the room required a reverence. Plus, she knew—and more than likely Nick did, too—that all he had to do was say one wrong word and she would be ready to argue with him again. But she didn't want that to happen, and she sensed he didn't, either, not here, not in this room with its generations of love, laughter and remembrances.

She glanced at him and saw a new heat glinting in his amber eyes. Damn. She could feel the heat on her skin and in her blood. It was clogging her lungs and fogging her mind.

Then he dropped his gaze to her breasts. "I don't remember that shirt looking as good on Kathie as it does on you."

His husky voice grated along her nerve endings, bringing even more heat. Automatically she looked. Her nipples were hard, their rigid tips clearly visible against the T-shirt. Color rushed to her cheeks.

Awkwardly she crossed her arms over her breasts so that her hands were on her upper arms. "Uh, did I miss some pictures? I didn't see any of your great-grandfather."

"There aren't any." He reached for her hands and pulled them away from her breasts. "Don't cover yourself."

If she stayed, something was going to happen that she didn't want to happen. She could feel it in her bones. The situation was too ripe for seduction, something she wasn't emotionally equipped to handle right now. Anger tangled with the heat, stress with the excitement of his nearness.

"You know, I think I can sleep now." Her heart was beating so hard, so loud, she could barely hear her own words.

"Liar," he whispered. "You could no more go to sleep now than I could."

"You're wrong. I could."

"I'm right. Besides, don't you want to hear more about the pictures?"

She hesitated. The insanity of it was that she *didn't* want to leave. "As long as we stay on the subject of the pictures."

He slowly smiled at her. "Okay. According to my grandfather, his father would never allow any pictures to be taken of himself."

"What about pictures of his wife and of your grandfather as a boy?"

He reached out for several strands of her hair and wound them around his fingers. "I like your hair loose and free."

She tried to move away, but his hold on her hair kept her close. "You're off the subject." Apparently the heat—in him, in her—had absorbed all the air in the room. She could barely breathe.

"So I am, and I'm sorry. But..." He rubbed the strands of hair between this thumb and fingers, as if fascinated by their texture.

She reached up and, as best she could, untangled her hair from his fingers. "The pictures?"

"The first picture ever made of my grandfather was on his wedding day. He was twenty-two years old."

"That's very sad."

"Yes, it is. In some ways, my grandfather led a very sad life, even a dark life, until the day he met my grandmother. Unfortunately, though, not even she could banish all the sadness of his childhood. It has stayed with him his entire life."

"That's a shame." She knew all about how a parent could color a child's existence. In fact, she knew more than she wanted to know. "Still, this room is a testament to a full life that was well lived. It must make them both feel good."

Deliberately she moved away from him. Heat, desire and passion permeated the air that surrounded him. Under the circumstances, she shouldn't be anywhere near him. But as she strolled to another part of the room, she could feel his gaze on her—that damn ability of his to touch her even when the length of a room separated them. It was an amazing skill, a dangerous skill.

"No matter what my grandparents have had to go

through in life, they've always had their love. To this day, they are as in love as they were on their wedding day. And you're right, theirs has been a life well lived. Unfortunately, according to the doctors, my grandmother will soon be alone. At this point, the doctors are not even sure what's keeping my grandfather alive.''

He paused. As she sensed he wanted her to, she looked at him. Then and only then did he go on. ''But Kathie and I know what it is. So does my grandmother. He's waiting for something to happen. He has a great will, my grandfather does.'' He shook his head in admiration. ''He's said he'll know when the end is near. And when the time comes, he wants us to bring him back out here so he can die in this place where he was born, and where his son was born, and where he raised Kathie and me.''

Tears filled her eyes, but she hastily blinked them away. ''I suppose a person couldn't ask for much more than to die in a place they love, surrounded by people who love them.''

''No, I don't suppose they could.''

She made her way to an old Victrola. A stack of records sat atop the lid, and she pulled off a few to read the labels. Except she couldn't really see the song titles. She was too overcome by the powerful emotions that this room and the people who had lived here had evoked in her. Damn it! She didn't even know them.

Obviously sadness had been a large part of Nick's grandparents' lives. For one thing, they'd lost their only son and daughter-in-law. But their pain hadn't stopped them from taking two small, hurting children into their home and life and spinning happiness and love around them until they felt safe and cared for. No matter what else, Nick's grandparents had a full grasp of what a family should be. It was something she'd never been taught.

By preserving this house, this room, Nick and his sister were returning their grandparents' love. And though Nick hadn't said so, she would bet this house would be kept just as it was now long after his grandparents had left this world.

In her family, love expressed or shown had always been in short supply. She'd been almost four when her mother had died. Jill had been just three, and Kit had been two. Their mother's early death had left the three of them to be raised solely by their father, a man who, if he had possessed any emotions, kept them to himself.

Sometimes, when she tried real hard, she could conjure up a memory of her mother tucking her into bed at night with a kiss and a hug. But she couldn't be sure if the memory was a true one or simply one she desperately wanted to be true.

Briefly she wondered if her life would have turned out differently if, after her mother's death, she'd been raised by people like Nick's grandparents. It was hard to say, and ultimately it didn't matter, anyway. If she'd learned nothing else from her father, she'd learned the uselessness of crying over spilt milk. She glanced at Nick who was leaning against the fireplace mantel, watching her.

"Why couldn't you sleep?" he asked, his voice carrying that same huskiness it had when she'd been standing beside him. "Is it because you're still angry at me?"

She replaced the records. "That and other things." It was all she was willing to say on the subject. Her anger and worry were justified, but anger didn't belong in this room, and her worries were none of Nick's concern. "I'm sorry if I woke you. I tried to be quiet when I came in here."

"I wasn't asleep, and I didn't hear you. I couldn't sleep, either."

"Why couldn't you sleep?" she asked softly, unable to resist the jab. "Guilt?"

The corners of his mouth turned upward in a rueful smile. "Maybe."

In the half darkness, in the silence, neither his face nor his body language gave her a clue as to what he was thinking. But if she'd had to guess, she would have said he was probably thinking of new ways to win her agreement to what he wanted of her.

She supposed she couldn't blame him. This room had given her a glimpse into what was driving him to recover the *Águila*'s treasure. It was family. Ironically, it was the same thing that was driving her to strike a Class-A oil field, and it was as vitally important to her as the air she breathed.

He broke the silence. "It's a long-standing habit of mine to come in here when I can't sleep. Even as a kid growing up, I'd come in here when I was having a restless night. Often I'd stay in here so long, I'd fall asleep right there on the couch. Then, sometime in the night, my grandmother would come in and cover me with one of her afghans. I'd wake up warm and rested."

And loved, she silently added. "I can understand why this room would have a soothing effect on you."

"Can you?"

Suddenly she remembered that she was wearing only a T-shirt. The fact that she'd forgotten in the last few minutes spoke volumes about how Nick and the room had affected her. Another few minutes and she would completely lose touch with reality. "I'm going back to my room now."

"Don't."

She looked at him in surprise. "Why?"

He made a vague gesture with his hand. "I could make us some hot chocolate, and we could talk some more."

*Hot chocolate and conversation with Nick.* Amazingly,

it was a much harder offer to turn down than it should have been, but she couldn't afford to hear any more about this room or Nick's family. She had to keep her mind on what was important to her rather than on what was important to Nick. Again, something surprisingly hard to do.

"No."

She didn't see him move, but suddenly he was in front of her. "Then how about this for a reason? Because I don't want to let you go just yet."

She tensed, ready to resist when he pulled her into his arms, but he surprised her yet again. He didn't. Instead he merely took a step and closed the distance between them.

"I should know better than this," he whispered, slowly lowering his mouth toward hers. "I should have learned after what happened between us in the kitchen." She could feel the breath of his words on her lips. "But you...there's you, and I don't know what to do about the way you make me feel."

She had plenty of time to move away or say no. But she did neither. She waited, listening, understanding. One moment the wanting wasn't there. The next it was. Inside her, full blown and impossible to ignore. And when finally his lips touched hers, she almost sighed with relief.

This kiss was unlike any other that he'd given her. It was unhurried and so gentle that she couldn't find any reason to resist. Their bodies were touching, but his hands weren't on her. And the pressure of his lips continued to be delicate, undemanding. Yet somehow, as he moved his mouth back and forth over hers, he still managed to find and awaken every nerve ending in her lips until heated sensations seeped through her, spreading, expanding.

She'd never experienced anything like it. He was only kissing her, yet she'd never been more aroused in her life. Her breasts began to ache. If only he would touch them.

Heat pooled between her legs until the area throbbed. If only he would put his hand there and stroke her, fill her....

She was in agony, but he continued at his own slow pace. His kisses remained gentle, as if he were memorizing every aspect of her lips—their shape, their softness. At that moment she actually felt as if she could die of need for him. Stifling a groan, she parted her lips. She had a fierce need to have him thrust his tongue deep into her mouth, but instead, he lightly nipped at the edges.

She swayed toward him. Her breasts with their rigid tips touched his bare chest, and she almost cried out at the pleasure that shot through her. It was a new kind of torture, and she could feel herself coming undone. Winding her arms around his neck, she stood on her tiptoes and pressed herself against him. Her body badly needed the contact. He was the source of incredible pleasure, and her body was craving it, him.

"Nick," she whispered, almost in pain, and threaded her fingers through his hair.

"Tell me," he whispered.

If her life had depended on it, she couldn't have expressed a clear thought. A low sound came out of her, saturated with frustration and need. Then his hand closed around her breast, and his thumb flicked her nipple. Fire scorched through her. Moaning, she closed her eyes and writhed against him.

Time became suspended as he backed her up until she felt the wall behind her; then he lifted her. Instinctively, she wrapped her legs around his hips and held on to him with all her might. His kisses turned harder, and at last his tongue delved deep and strong into her mouth. His hand slid beneath the T-shirt and this time closed around her bare breast. It was what she'd been wanting, needing, but she couldn't even enjoy it, because by this point she wanted more, so much more.

Feelings were rapidly closing down all thought, but some distant part of her brain was still working. Her body was vibrating with a crucial need for satisfaction, and in another few moments Nick would give it to her, but...

She felt him lift her bottom, adjust his stance, then he was pressing harder against her at the juncture of her thighs. Denim rubbed back and forth against silk panties. His hips rotated and thrust against her sensitive, pulsing flesh beneath the silk.

Oh, she wanted this. She *needed* this. And she could have it. Just another minute, less. But...what would be the cost to her? Her fingers tightened in his hair. "Stop." The word wasn't a whisper, more an amalgamation of feelings and sounds. She didn't even know what part of her it had come from, and in the next moment, she wished for it back.

Nick halted all movement. A hard shudder violently racked his body. "Did you say stop?" His voice was broken, hoarse, pain-filled.

"No. No. Oh, Nick. I want you so badly.... But...please help me."

An agonized noise rumbled from his chest. Slowly, with tremors shaking his whole body, he eased both of them away from the wall. At first she wasn't certain she had the willpower or the strength to let him go. She waited. Finally she managed to unwrap her legs from around him.

He dropped his hands away until the only thing holding her to him was her arms around his neck, but once again, she had trouble letting him go, yet she knew she had to. Doing her best not to meet his eyes, she loosened her hold, and her arms fell to her side.

Breathing in great gulps of air, Nick stepped away from her and turned his back to her.

She felt sick to her stomach. Her body was on fire, but there would be no satisfaction for her throbbing body. Worse, she had no idea what to say, and she was embarrassed beyond words.

"Nick... "

"Don't say anything. Not now." He held up his hand. "I'm sorry, Tess. I let it go too far."

"Only because I wanted you to. At the very least, fifty percent of the blame goes to me."

Shakily she started for the door, then thought of something. "Will I be able to hear the phone if it rings?" After what had just happened between them, she felt ludicrous asking the question. Or, for that matter, even thinking of it. Maybe it was her mind's way of trying to protect her, taking her thoughts away from her hurting body and putting them on business. If so, it wasn't working.

Without turning to face her, he nodded. "There's a phone in the hall. Unless you're a very heavy sleeper, you'll be able to hear it."

She stared at his back, searching her mind for something to say that would make the past fifteen minutes go away. But there were no words adequate enough to accomplish that feat.

From the start, the deck had been stacked against them. They'd both been half-dressed, in a half-lit room, with too much bare skin, too many raw emotions and too much sexual attraction.

She wrapped her arms around her waist, trying to stop herself from shaking. She didn't know why it was so important to her for him to turn around and look at her, but it was. So she asked him another question, a question that should have been left unasked. "And you haven't switched off the phone?"

"Check it yourself," he snapped, a man on the edge. "It's on."

"Okay. " She hesitated, then reached for the doorknob. "Good night."

"Tess?"

Her heart jumped. She looked to find that he'd finally turned to face her. "Yes?"

"I wish things could be different."

She knew exactly what he meant. His treasure. Her oil well. It was a stalemate.

Without answering, she opened the door to the hall, then quietly closed it behind her. Back in her room, back in the bed, she stared at the ceiling. Nick would never know how much she'd wanted to stay with him or how hard it had been for her to walk out. But staying would have been too dangerous.

Whether they were angry at each other or talking about something as innocuous as family pictures, they struck sparks off each other. And sparks, if not controlled, led to fire. She only had to look at him to want him. And when he kissed her, she came apart in his arms.

Somewhere in the house she heard water come on. She didn't have to think twice to know Nick was taking a cold shower. She wished for one for herself.

God, if she could just get home tomorrow, whole and without a broken heart, she would consider herself incredibly lucky.

# Five

Tess slowly awoke to the warmth of sunshine on her face and the delicious aroma of coffee. A glance out the window told her it was going to be a beautiful day.

Amazingly, considering the events of the previous night, she'd slept remarkably well. Then again, maybe it wasn't so amazing. In that dimly lit room with Nick, her emotions had run the gamut from anger to passion, emotions so powerful they'd rocked her world and left her spent. By the time she'd crawled into bed, she'd felt as if she'd been put through a meat grinder.

And she had only herself to blame. She'd been incredibly stupid for accepting a date with Nick, even though deep down she'd known the real reason he'd asked her out. And she'd been stupid for getting on a plane with him even though she'd felt uneasy about it. But most of all, she'd been stupid for wanting him as much as she had last night.

Soon, though, it would be over. She just had to get past

meeting Nick's grandparents, and then she would be on her way home to her usual life. Then maybe, just maybe, this strange mixture of dread and uneasiness in her stomach would go away.

The phone rang. *Ron.* She leaped out of bed and ran toward the hall phone, but before she could reach it, it stopped ringing. She hurried into the kitchen to find Nick with the receiver to his ear, listening.

"Is it for me?" she asked.

Shaking his head, he continued to listen to whoever had called.

She watched him, wondering what or who had him looking so serious. He wasn't wearing a shirt; his hair was wet and tousled, and she could see droplets of water clinging to the fine black hair that covered his chest. He must have just showered.

*She would love to lick him dry.*

The thought came from nowhere and nearly knocked her to her knees. She swallowed hard. She couldn't allow those kinds of thoughts. Last night, that room, what had happened there between them…it had all been a piece of time away from the real world, away from reality. It wouldn't happen again. It couldn't.

Her gaze continued down his body to his hip-hugging jeans. They weren't the same jeans he'd worn last night, but…they were zipped, but not yet buttoned.

*Oh, God…* She felt her blood begin to warm. Before Nick had arrived in her life, she would never have thought she could be capable of such thoughts and feelings. She walked over to the counter and poured herself a cup of coffee.

To the uninformed, she speculated, they could easily be mistaken for lovers who had awakened together after a night of passion. She was in the same T-shirt she'd slept in.

And if it *were* true, if they had indeed slept together after a night of lovemaking, she knew without thinking twice that she would be feeling completely satisfied this morning. In fact, she probably wouldn't have a nerve left in her body.

Her hand flew to her forehead. She had to stop thinking about things like that, things that would never happen, could never happen.

"How bad is it?" she heard him ask and forced her attention to his end of the call. "And the doctor is sure?" He paused, then smiled. "That sounds like him. So okay, then—" he glanced at her "—that's what we'll do if at all possible. Be sure and call if anything changes." He nodded. "Right, I'll let you know. Give the girls a kiss and a hug for me and save a couple for yourself. Bye, honey."

He hung up the phone, then leveled his amber gaze on her. "That was Kathie. Our grandfather had a bad spell this morning."

"I'm sorry to hear that." It was the truth, she realized, sipping her coffee. Because of the pictures she'd seen last night, she felt as if she already knew him. "But now that our visit is obviously off, I'll get ready and we can head back to Corpus as soon as possible."

"My grandfather wants to meet you very badly, Tess. He's requested that we come later on this afternoon, when he thinks he'll be feeling better."

"I hope he is, but I can't afford to waste any more time."

Muscle by muscle, he tensed. It was something she sensed, but if she'd had her hands on his body, she couldn't have felt it any better. And the amber of his eyes darkened to an intensity and a sharpness that could have cut a dia-

mond. "Is that what this has been to you? Truly? Just a
big waste of time?"

She couldn't truthfully say that. She'd wanted to learn
more about him, and she had. But perhaps more importantly, she'd also learned something about herself that she'd
never known. Last night, looking at the pictures in the living room, she'd realized that she badly wanted a close,
loving family, something she'd never had and probably
never would have.

"This morning starts a new day," she said carefully,
averting her eyes to her coffee cup, "and it's a day I badly
need to spend back in Corpus." She paused and looked at
him. "I'm sorry, but I just can't wait around all day to see
your grandfather."

He ran an agitated hand through his hair. "Look, I know
that all you have to do is pick up the phone and call your
assistant. He'll be in the office by now, and he could have
a plane chartered, arrange for a car on this end and have
you home by noon, but—"

"Calling him is exactly what I intend to do. Last night
he must have slept over at his girlfriend's, so he didn't get
my message. But by now, he'll be at work."

And as soon as she got back to Corpus, she planned to
tell him that from now on, no matter where he spent the
night, he was to call the office and check his messages.

"Please, Tess, just listen to me for a minute."

"Don't say please to me ever again." She slammed her
cup on the counter with enough force that coffee sloshed
everywhere. It was a wonder the cup hadn't broken.

"I'll get down on my knees and beg you if it would
help. Tess, my grandfather is dying, and meeting you is
important to him."

She could feel herself beginning to weaken. *Damn it.*
Giving in to his requests was how she'd gotten herself into

this mess in the first place. "Why, Nick? Does he, or do you, actually think hearing the story from a dying man will change my mind? It can't. Don't you understand? *It can't.*"

"No, Tess. I don't understand. I'm only asking for a postponement of a few months. At the end of that time, the oil will still be there. It's not going anywhere."

She sighed. So after all that had transpired last night, they were right back to the basics. He wanted something from her, and she couldn't give it to him. "There are reasons I can't stop the drilling."

"Tell me."

He'd said *tell me* last night when, in the heat of passion, she had moaned his name. But then he hadn't really needed her to tell him what she'd wanted. He'd known. "My reasons are private."

Tense silence charged the air. Praying for composure, she went about cleaning up the spill, then poured herself more coffee.

"Okay, Tess," he said, his tone gruff. "Forget about what I want. Think about my grandfather, instead. He's going to be very disappointed if he doesn't get to meet you." She opened her mouth to speak, but he rushed on. "And not only because you have the power to stop the drilling. He's heard me talk about you and—"

"What do you mean, he's heard you talk about me? We only met two nights ago."

"I did a little research on you before we met."

"So you said before."

"The library and years of microfiche clued me in to a few things, but basically, family-owned businesses such as yours are very secretive. But you...your name and picture came up quite a few times, both in the business section of the paper and the society section."

"And what does that have to do with your grandfather?"

He slowly exhaled. "Even before you and I met, he told me that my tone of voice changed when I was talking about you. And after we met, he said that even though I've mentioned quite a few women to him over the years, he's never heard this particular tone in my voice before. He says it's clear that I'm attracted to you. He's lived to see Kathie happily married and settled, and he has just about decided that…that you will be the one I'll marry."

Her heart jumped into her throat. "He must have a spectacularly vivid imagination."

His eyes thoughtfully narrowed on her. "I suppose so. But you have to remember that he's dying. From his viewpoint, he's afraid he won't live to see me married. So now he's decided that the next best thing is to meet the woman he thinks has won my heart. As I said, he's very excited about your visit this afternoon."

She stared at him, her mind busy absorbing the newest surprise he'd pulled out of his hat for her. "But that's ridiculous."

"Not to him," he said, his tone very firm. "So you see, this visit involves much more than the *Águila* and its safety. You would be doing me a great favor if you would wait until after you've visited with him to leave."

"You don't fight fair."

"I never said I did."

She put a hand to her forehead, where she could feel pressure beginning to build. "I have to think about this." With her coffee cup, she turned to go to her bedroom.

"Would you like some breakfast? I can make just about anything."

She didn't even glance back at him. "No, thank you."

Tess showered, soaping her body and shampooing her hair. Then she simply stood beneath the water and let it rain down over her. It was wonderful.

She forced herself to concentrate only on the water and to think about nothing else. Too many things had happened too fast. Her mind needed a rest. And her body... Unfortunately, it needed much more.

But it didn't matter. Telling Nick to stop last night had been the best thing she could have done. It really had been, she assured herself. She was already more involved with him than she should be.

Physically, she'd gone way too far with him. Emotionally, she was all tangled up in him *and* his family, whom she had yet to meet. Figure that one out, she told herself ruefully, as she leaned against the tiles and allowed the water to sluice over her. She couldn't.

She climbed out, dried off and dressed in her red sleeveless dress. Her hair was wet, but she hadn't been able to find a hair dryer, so she decided to let it dry naturally.

In order to avoid Nick, she went out the front door.

The day was warm, with only a slight breeze. She could see the wonderful scenery she'd missed last night. The hills were white with caliche. Thickets of mesquite and wild grasses tangled in the eroded ravines. Yellow and red blooms on the prickly pears clumped in the bar ditch, indicating a recent rain. And the vine that everyone called Grandpa's beard wrapped itself around the fences and telephone poles, each petal a silvery white.

Nick's grandparents might not own that many acres, but what they did own was beautiful. She made her way around the house and saw cattle grazing in a distant meadow. Closer to the house, she spied a swing hung in a gazebo. On three sides, the junipers grew thick around it and would filter the air.

Nice. She imagined that Nick's grandparents had probably spent many evenings right there, discussing the events of the day and their grandchildren. And the fact that she had even thought of that worried her.

She settled into the swing and lifted her face for the cooling breeze. What was she going to do? Nick didn't have a clue what she was up against, and even if he did, he would never agree that what she had to accomplish was more important than the dreams of his dying grandfather.

She couldn't blame him for that. But... She closed her eyes and shook her head in bemusement at the decision she was about to make.

But she supposed that since she was already here, the least she could do was to stay and meet Nick's grandfather. He believed Nick was in love with her, and even though nothing could be further from the truth, she couldn't find it in herself to disillusion him. She sighed. She hadn't even met the man, but here she was, trying to make him happy.

Making a dying man happy was a big responsibility. It was also an unfair responsibility, imposed on her by Nick. But because of the pictures, she would stay and do her best.

"May I join you?"

Her eyes flew open. Outlined against the blue sky, surrounded by brilliant sunshine, dressed in a gold knit polo shirt, Nick appeared every bit the sun god she'd first thought him to be.

In the incredibly short time she'd known him, he'd turned her life completely upside down. She'd gazed into his amber eyes and, like a lamb, had followed him wherever he had led her. She'd made not only bad decisions, she was now making bewildering decisions.

And at that moment, looking at him, all the hunger and need she'd felt for him last night came flooding back. Damn it. Somehow, in some way, she had to make those feelings go away for good. The sooner she was in her office, dealing with problems that she knew how to handle, the better off she would be.

"Actually, yes. I have a question for you." He started to sit beside her, but she quickly held up her hand. "I'd prefer it if you didn't sit here."

He stared at her for several moments. "Okay." His slid one hand into his jeans pocket and, with the other, gripped the swing's chain.

Briefly she considered the very real possibility that she'd made a mistake in telling him not to sit beside her. As it was, her eyes were even with the waistband of his jeans. Thankfully he'd buttoned them, but with very little effort, she knew her gaze could wander downward and her imagination could take flight with thoughts of what was behind that fly. Truthfully, it wouldn't take a lot of imagination. She'd felt it last night as he'd moved against her....

Her mouth went suddenly dry. "The night we met, you said that somehow you thought you had a chance at convincing me to give you the needed time. Why?"

"I thought you'd understand about a man who'd had one dream his whole life."

"I assume you're talking about your grandfather, but why would you think I would understand his dream?"

"I've already told you that I'd done a bit of homework on you. In the course of my reading, I found several articles on the Dream Foundation that you've established for underprivileged children."

She nodded. "I've always thought that just because a child comes from a poor background doesn't mean that they shouldn't have a way to follow their dreams. And in my foundation, the words *underprivileged* and *poor* can mean many things. Maybe a child comes from a family who has money, but they belittle the child's dream, or give that child no emotional support. My foundation tries to reach those children, too.''

''Exactly. My thought was that if you had the ability to understand that children need help in making their dreams come true, you would also understand that some adults have the same need.''

He'd cornered her by using her own beliefs against her. Very neat. Very sharp. ''I *can* understand that, but in this case...'' She cleared her throat. ''In this case, it isn't possible to grant any part of what you're asking.''

''Why?''

''You've already asked that question, and I've already told you the reason is private.'' By unspoken agreement, no one in their family ever talked to any outsider about its dynamics, and she wasn't going to be the first. ''Just because I have autonomy over my section of Baron International doesn't mean I don't have pressures and responsibilities that involve the family. You have to understand from our initial surveys and core samplings, it looks as if this particular well has the potential to bring in millions per year.''

''So will my gold, though of course not for years. But I'm not doing this for the money. Even though my family has proof that we legally own that gold, the State of Texas will still get its slice, the backers will get their slices, and I'll donate most of the antiquities to the university.'' He shrugged. ''Then, after the Internal Revenue Service takes its bite, there'll be something left over for my grandparents, if they're still alive. If not, it will be divided between Kathie and me. But the money isn't the point and never has been.''

He released the swing's chain and squatted in front of her, his forearms resting on his thighs, his hands clasped, two fingers held together in a point. ''Look, Tess, I'm not saying my problems are more important than your problems. I'm just saying that I've got a time crunch. And right now will be my *only* chance.''

''Why? As you said about my oil, your treasure isn't going anywhere. What happens at my well may disturb your treasure, but you'll still know its general area.''

''*Now* is when I have to act. After years of trying to make it happen, now is when everything has come together. I have my backers lined up, and believe me, getting backers for such a speculative venture was not easy. I've also got the people lined up who will be working with me to harvest the gold, along with the machinery. But if my backers get a whiff of any delay or difficulty, they may very well withdraw their money. Then I'd have to start all over again from the beginning, and that could take years.''

''Your backers don't know about my drilling site?''

He shook his head. ''And, if possible, I've got to keep it that way. I can't afford for them to start getting nervous. It took me years to get some of these people to commit, and at that time I knew nothing about your plans. So now what I'm doing is lying to them by omission. And as you pointed out last night, a lie of omission is still a lie. You may not believe it, but I rarely lie. I don't feel exactly great about keeping my backers in the dark, but that's how desperate I am to keep them committed to my project. And that's how immediate my need is. You've got to stop drilling *now*, Tess. Because if you continue drilling, and if something happens to send the *Águila* over that salt ridge, it will be buried so deeply, it may very well be lost for all time, or at least for my generation.''

Once again, that now familiar pressure band was beginning to squeeze her head. There was really nothing she could say to Nick. He could never understand what she was up against or how every day was a struggle for her. Nor

would he understand how and why her every waking minute was spent trying to fulfill her deceased father's goals
for her, and there was no reason he should. There was also
no reason she should try to make him understand. Soon he
would be gone from her life.

The phone rang in the house. Nick took off at a slow
jog to answer it. With a sigh, she stood and rubbed her
temples, then remembered she'd forgotten to call Ron.

Nick met her at the back door. "It's for you. He said to
tell you it's Des."

Des? *Oh, God. Uncle William.* She raced to the phone.
"Des? What's wrong? Is it Uncle William?"

"No," he answered, his voice deep and even. "He's
fine. I'm calling about you."

"Me?" she asked, astonished. It was a rare day when
Des called her. "What about me?"

"Your disappearance. Tell me right now—are you in
trouble? Are you being held against your will?"

She glanced at Nick, who was listening intently. "No."

"Okay, good. What happened was this. Ron didn't sleep
at your house last night, but when he showed up for work
this morning, he found your message on the machine. It
said you needed help and to please call you back as soon
as possible. But you didn't leave him a number."

"I didn't?" She pressed the heel of her hand to her forehead. Had she forgotten to give Ron the number because
she'd been so agitated? Or was the reason more basic? A
Freudian slip? "I can't believe I did that. But there's always my cell phone."

"Which he found on your bed, when he searched the
house."

"Right." She remembered tossing it there right before
she walked out the door. Damn.

"So Ron questioned the staff, and they all said you had

# Play The *Lucky Hearts* Game

## and get...
## FREE BOOKS, a FREE GIFT...
## and MUCH more!

*Yes!* I have scratched off the silver card. Please send me my **2 FREE BOOKS** and **FREE MYSTERY GIFT**. I understand that I am under no obligation to purchase any books as explained on the back of this card.

**Scratch Here!**
then look below to see what your cards get you...

**326 SDL CTJL**

**225 SDL CTJD**

Name _____
(PLEASE PRINT)

Address _____ Apt.#

City _____ State/Prov. _____ Postal Zip/Code

Twenty-one gets you **2 FREE BOOKS** and a **FREE MYSTERY GIFT!**

Twenty gets you **2 FREE BOOKS!**

Nineteen gets you **1 FREE BOOK!**

**TRY AGAIN!**

Offer limited to one per household and not valid to current Silhouette Desire® subscribers. All orders subject to approval.

PRINTED IN U.S.A.

## The Silhouette Reader Service™ — Here's how it works:

Accepting your 2 free books and mystery gift places you under no obligation to buy anything. You may keep the books and gift and return the shipping statement marked "cancel." If you do not cancel, about a month later we'll send you 6 additional novels and bill you just $3.12 each in the U.S., or $3.49 each in Canada, plus 25¢ delivery per book and applicable taxes if any.* That's the complete price and — compared to the cover price of $3.75 in the U.S. and $4.25 in Canada — it's quite a bargain! You may cancel at any time, but if you choose to continue, every month we'll send you 6 more books, which you may either purchase at the discount price or return to us and cancel your subscription.

*Terms and prices subject to change without notice. Sales tax applicable in N.Y. Canadian residents will be charged applicable provincial taxes and GST.

left last night on a date and hadn't returned. Ron became alarmed, and rightly so. So he called me.''

"I see. But how on earth were you able to track me down?''

"I had a little luck on my side. First of all, Guadalupe described your date, and from the description, Ron was able to identify him as Nick Trejo. Still, if Trejo had stayed in town, I probably wouldn't have been able to track you down. Same thing if he'd chosen to drive you to Uvalde. But because he chose to fly, it was a little easier. I called the airport and made inquiries until I found someone who had recognized you getting on a private plane. Then all I had to do was track down the flight plan and call Uvalde information.''

"You went to a lot of trouble, Des. I'm sorry.''

"If you had left a number for Ron and he had called you back last night, what help would you have asked him for?''

"I would have asked him to charter a plane and come and get me.''

"Did you know when you left the house yesterday evening that you were going to Uvalde and wouldn't be home last night?''

She glanced at Nick, who was regarding her solemnly. "No, I didn't. It was a...surprise.''

"And obviously not a welcome one, since you wanted to leave so badly.''

"Right.''

"In other words, you were kidnapped.''

"You could say that, yes, but—''

"I'll come get you. Give me the address where you are.''

She hesitated. If she'd tried, she couldn't have planned a better way to trick Des into spending time with her. He was actually offering to come to her rescue. If she agreed, it would give her at least a couple of hours alone with him, which was exactly what she'd yearned for the night before last. But today... "That won't be necessary, Des. I'm staying until this afternoon to meet Nick's grandparents."

"Of your own free will?"

"Yes. And afterward, Nick will fly me home."

"Are you sure you don't want me to come get you now?"

She closed her eyes, having a hard time believing she was going to turn him down. "Yes, I'm sure."

"And if he decides to keep you there another night?"

Her eyes opened and she looked at Nick. She couldn't tell what he was thinking. "He won't, but if he tries, I'll call you. Wait a minute. Give me the number where you are." She pantomimed a pencil and paper to Nick, and he quickly produced them. "Okay, Des, what's the number?" She wrote it down. "Thanks. I promise I'll call if I need you."

"Just to be safe, call me this evening when you get home."

She was nearly stunned into speechlessness. He sounded as if he cared about her. Not romantically, but in a way that made it seem as if she mattered to him. "Are you sure? I mean, Ron could contact you again if I don't get home. And if you don't hear from him, then you'll know I'm home. That would be less trouble for you."

"I don't mind this kind of trouble. If you're in trouble, Tess, never hesitate to call. You're family."

For a moment she thought she'd misunderstood him. He'd never said anything remotely like that before. More often than not, Des seemed to go to great lengths to avoid her and her sisters. "Thank you. I appreciate this more than I can say."

"No problem. Talk to you this evening."

"Right." She hung up.

"Who is this Des, and why does he think you need rescuing?"

She turned to face Nick. "Oh, I don't know, Nick. Probably because I did need rescuing."

"Did?"

"Last night. If you'll remember, I *did* want to leave."

"You were never in danger."

No, she reflected. Not the type of physical danger he meant. "There's no point in arguing about it now. I'll be home by this evening."

"You didn't answer part of my question. Who is Des?"

"He's the son of my aunt May from her first marriage. When she and my father's brother, Uncle William, married, Uncle William adopted Des. Uncle William and Aunt May never had any other children."

"So the night of your birthday party, why were your two sisters so anxious for him to be there?"

"Just a game we play."

"A game?"

She shook her head. "It's complicated."

"And you don't think I'm smart enough to grasp the complexities?"

"Let's just drop it, okay? I don't want to talk about it."

"Okay." He studied her. "Is Des satisfied now that you're in no danger?"

"You heard me tell him that you would fly me home this evening."

He crossed his arms over his chest. "And do you believe that I will?"

"Yes."

"And what if I don't?"

"I'll call Des, and he'll come get me."

"And what if I ask you to stay?"

She paused for a moment to insure that her tone of voice

was as casual as she could manage. She wanted him to believe she saw his question as involving his grandfather or the *Águila*. She didn't want him to bring up the personal or know that her mind had gone straight to the image of him holding her against the wall, with her legs wrapped around him, wanting him with every molecule of her being. "Why would you do that? I've agreed to stay and meet your grandparents. After that, you will have accomplished what you set out to do by bringing me here."

A volatile silence filled the room; she had the feeling that if she lit a match, the whole place would explode into flames.

Finally he spoke. "So that's the way you want to play it? As if, last night, nothing at all unusual happened between us?"

She clasped her suddenly shaking hands together and looked down at them. "I think that's best. I mean, it happened, but it was a product of the night and the place."

"That's pure *bull* and you know it."

"Then let me put it this way. There's nothing that could come from it. You want something I can't give you, Nick. That's the beginning, middle and end of our relationship. The fact that I can't agree to what you want will taint anything else."

"Damn it, Tess. Last night, right here in this kitchen, I told you I wanted you. And then later—"

"Later we almost made a terrible mistake. I stopped it because there is no future for you and me."

"And there's no trust, right?"

She looked at him. "Trust?"

"Let's put the cards on the table. If we made love, you would think I was trying to seduce you into doing what I want. And me? Maybe I'd think you were trying to get my focus off the *Águila,* to make me want you so badly that I'd forget any and everything but you.''

She felt herself pale. The first part was true. She had thought that. As for the second part—there was no way she could ever believe that, by having sex with him, she could make him forget anything.

''But,'' he said, his voice soft, ''knowing all that doesn't make the wanting go away, does it, Tess?''

No, damn it, it didn't. She felt as if she was frantically juggling, trying to keep all her various balls in the air—the tenuous hold she had on her emotions when it came to Nick, her work and its time crunch, not to mention her future, her rivalry with her sisters, Des and, strangely enough, the compassion she felt for Nick's grandfather. And she was convinced that if she let just one ball drop, they would all drop, and she would lose everything.

Waiting for her in Corpus was a long list of things that only she could make decisions on. The well being drilled in the Gulf of Mexico, while vitally important to her, was by no means her only concern. The rest of her business continued. Her piece of the Baron pie, while being only one-sixth, was enormous, which, in turn, brought enormous responsibilities.

More immediate was the upcoming visit with Nick's grandparents. She didn't think for a minute that it would be easy.

And Des. He had called her out of the blue, worried about her, offering to rescue her like a knight on a white horse. It would have been a perfect opportunity for her to blindside her sisters and attempt to get him to look at her not just as family but as a desirable woman. But she'd let it pass. Even more bizarre was the fact that she didn't even want to think about why she'd turned him down. Not now, at any rate.

She was much too busy trying to keep some sort of emotional balance with Nick. But later, she told herself, she would think about her reason. Later, when she got home and felt on safer ground, she would think about it. Later...

And last, but certainly not least, she had Nick telling her he wanted her, then laying out the reasons they both knew should keep them from making love. But as he'd said, the reasons didn't make the wanting go away.

At the moment, it was just one ball too many for her. "I need to get back to Corpus Christi this evening, Nick. And if you won't take me, I'll find another way."

"That won't be necessary. I'll take you."

# Six

Frail arms warmly enfolded Tess in a hug; then Nick's grandmother stepped back and beamed at her. "How lovely to meet you, my dear."

"Thank you, Mrs. Trejo. It's nice to meet you, too."

"Oh, please, call me Alma. We don't stand on formalities around here."

"Alma, then."

Alma was a tiny lady, wearing navy polyester pants with a neatly ironed pink flowered blouse. Her gray hair was cut short in a soft, flattering style, and her skin had its share of wrinkles, both from age and, Tess guessed, the Texas sun. Alma's wedding picture flashed into Tess's head. It had shown a pretty but shy young woman, shining with happiness and hope. Today Alma no longer seemed shy, but the happiness was still with her, along with the hope.

Amazing, she reflected. Alma had suffered a hard life and had known the pain of losing a son. Now she had to cope with the knowledge that her husband might not be with her much longer. In addition, she had health problems herself. Yet she hadn't lost the capability of feeling happiness and hope.

Remarkable.

Alma's brown eyes sparkled with pleasure. "Now come over here and meet Ben. He's been waiting all day for this."

"Damn right," a breathy voice said. "Come over here, Tess, and let me get a look at you."

She followed the voice to a hospital bed set up in an alcove where a big bay window offered a view of flowers, trees and a sky so blue it looked as if it had been painted. On the window ledge there was a picture. In the center of it, Nick's grandfather was sitting in a chair. Nick and Alma stood on one side of him, Kathie and her husband on the other, and two little girls sat on the grass at their great-grandfather's feet. Another important picture to add to the legacy of their family.

"Mr. Trejo?" She held out her hand to the wizened old man, who was breathing with the aid of oxygen.

He shook her hand with surprising strength. "Ben. Name's Ben. Nick, pull her up a chair so I can talk to this pretty young lady."

Without a word, Nick did as his grandfather asked and motioned to Tess to sit down.

"I'll be right back with some iced tea for all of us," Alma said, still beaming.

Tess started to say she didn't want anything, but Alma had already disappeared. She returned her attention to Ben. "How are you feeling? I understand you had something of a bad spell this morning."

Ben waved a dismissive hand. "It was nothin'. No matter what the doc says, I'm not ready to go yet."

"That's good to hear." She'd started off with pleasantries, but from here on out, she decided, it would be best to let him lead the conversation.

"Nick, come rearrange my pillows so I can sit up straighter."

"You're at the angle your doctor wants you to be, Grandpa."

"Damn it, Nick." Ben looked at Tess. "You know you're old when your pup of a grandson won't do what you say."

Nick grinned. "Your pup of a grandson is only trying to keep you alive for as long as possible."

Ben made a disgruntled sound. "Go off someplace and leave us alone. Tess, you and I need to have a nice long visit."

She smiled. It was easy to envision this old man whose life was drawing to an end as a virile, vital young man. She only had to look at Nick to see the likeness. "I'd like that."

For the very first time she was happy she'd given in to Nick and stayed long enough to meet Alma and Ben. She saw now that Nick hadn't been exaggerating when he'd said they wanted to meet her. There was no doubt they would have been very disappointed if she hadn't come. But she also had the odd feeling that somehow her life would have been diminished if she'd missed meeting them. Funny thing to feel, but true.

Despite his grandfather's order to leave, Nick, she noticed, had drawn up a chair at the other side of the bed and settled into it.

Ben's fingers absently moved on the sheet. His hands and arms were dry and wrinkled. At the bend of his elbow were purple and yellow bruises, probably from myriad needle pricks. "Nick's told you about his find, hasn't he?"

"If you mean that he's found your father's gold, yes, he has."

Tears moistened Ben's milky eyes. "I never thought it would happen. In fact, I didn't think it was possible." Silently Nick rose and handed his grandfather his handkerchief, but the old man didn't bother to use it. "I can't tell you how much I wish Papa was alive today. It would mean the world to him."

"Yes, I'm sure it would." She tried to keep her response as neutral as possible and avoided looking at Nick. Nevertheless, she could feel his gaze trained on her, and she sensed he was ready to pounce if she said anything to upset Ben.

The old man shook his head. "No one knows. No one knows." He blinked the moisture from his eyes. "After the ship sank with the gold, Papa's life just went to hell. He'd dreamed of a ranch the size of the Briscoe or even the King. Instead he had to settle for a few measly acres and a lifetime of ridicule."

"Ridicule?" She hadn't meant to ask him anything that would encourage him to continue with something that obviously upset him, but the word just popped out.

"No one would believe Papa when he told them how he'd mined a fortune of gold but lost it in a hurricane. They ridiculed him, and Papa...well, he was a proud man, way too proud, Mama always said. But knowing that people felt he was nothin' but a joke sliced him up all inside." He paused and wiped his eyes.

"Don't overdo, Grandpa." Nick's soft voice revealed concern.

Ben didn't appear to hear him. "Somehow Mama was able to get through to him and show him what real kindness and love were all about. And at least he had the good sense to marry her. Of course, her parents were mad as hornets about it, but Mama was every bit as determined as Papa was proud, and she got her way. Still, as the years went on, he just got worse and worse, all locked up inside himself.''

"Grandpa, take it easy. Getting upset is not going to do you any good."

Ben waved him away. "Didn't I tell you to go someplace?"

Nick settled into his chair as Alma walked in carrying two glasses of tea. She handed one to Tess and the other to Nick. "The mint came from my own garden, Tess."

Alma waited expectantly while Tess took a sip. "It's delicious. Thank you."

Alma's smile lit up her face.

"Where's mine?" Ben asked hoarsely.

"I only have two hands, now, don't I? I'll be bringing yours next."

Ben looked at Tess, and she was surprised to see a twinkle in his eyes. "Another way you know you're old is when you have to drink decaffeinated tea without much sugar."

"Don't listen to him, honey," Alma said. "He only knows it's decaffeinated with just a pinch of sugar because I told him. The truth is, the way I fix it, he can't tell the difference."

"So she says." When Alma left the room, Ben winked at Tess. "I let her think I can't, but the truth is, I really can."

Tess couldn't help but smile. "How long have you two been married?"

"Nearly sixty years."

"That's wonderful," she said sincerely. What was especially wonderful to her was the obvious and deep love they still had for each other. She'd never before had the

chance to witness that type of durable love that had lasted
through good times and bad.

"Now, let's see, where was I?"

"You were telling me about your father."

"Oh, yes, Papa." Ben's gaze drifted toward the window,
as if it were a movie screen and he was seeing scenes from
long ago. "Well, you know how it is, Tess. Kids can be
so cruel. They'd hear their papas talking about mine, and
they'd say the same things to me. They'd throw stuff at
me, rocks and such. To them, we were both crazy, but when
it came down to fightin', I gave 'bout as good as I got.
Still, they made it so that I could never belong. They had
a baseball team that I really wanted to play on, but..."

With a shrug, he focused on her. "A lot of those kids
are still alive today, and now that Nick has found the ship
and the gold, I swear I'm going to live long enough for
him to bring up a sizable amount. I want him to stack the
bullion in the middle of town, so those men who used to
throw rocks at me can see it and know how wrong they
were. I want them to know that my papa didn't lie and that
I didn't deserve the way they treated me."

The tears that sprang into her eyes surprised her. She
quickly brushed them away. "I'm so sorry."

"Well, now, there's nothing for you to be sorry about."
He gazed at her for several seconds. "Nick tells me you
might stop your drilling for us."

For the first time, she looked at Nick, but his expression
remained impassive. "Mm, yes, I'm considering it." What
else could she say?

Ben nodded. "I'm very grateful to you for that. I know
I don't have long to live. I also know I don't understand
the ins and outs of the world anymore or what you young
people have to face in your business lives. But if you could

see your way clear to do this for us, it would mean the earth to both Alma and me.''

Frantically she searched her mind for a noncommittal reply. A glance at Nick told her that he wasn't going to help her out. But Alma saved her by appearing with Ben's tea. ''Here you are, sweetheart. Just how you like it.''

''Thank you, honey. Now sit down and get acquainted with Tess. She's not only pretty as a picture, she's an awful nice girl.''

Alma laughed. ''I never doubted that for a minute. After all, Nick's taken quite a fancy to her, and we both know what good taste he has.''

Tess glanced at Nick, but he wasn't giving anything away.

Alma looked at her husband and apparently didn't like what she saw. ''I've got an idea. Tess, why don't you come out to the garden with me? We'll pick some flowers so that I can send you home with a lovely bouquet.''

Ben's brows rose slightly. ''Don't overdo it, Alma.''

Nick stood. ''I'll take Tess.''

Alma waved her hand. ''Sit down, Nick, and, Ben, relax. I'm taking her out to the garden, and that's that.'' She turned toward her. ''Come on, sweetheart.''

With a grin, Nick sat down. ''You might as well go, Tess. No one can change my grandmother's mind once she gets an idea.''

Tess rose and followed Alma.

''I hope you don't mind that we came out here,'' Alma said as soon as she shut the door of the house behind her. ''I could tell Ben was overdoing it and needed a little rest.''

''I don't mind at all.'' She remembered that Ben had told his wife not to overdo. What would it be like, she wondered, to have a husband who loved you so much that he worried about your well-being even after sixty years?

She could think of no one who worried about her well-being in that way, though Des had been ready to come get her when he thought she was in danger. *Des*. Something was bothering her about her decision to turn down his offer, an offer that only a few days ago she would have moved heaven and earth to get. Later, she reminded herself. Later she would think about it.

"I had a much larger garden out at our home," Alma said as they walked toward the relatively small but nevertheless pretty beds of blooming perennials and annuals.

"I stayed at your home last night. It's a wonderful place."

Once again Alma beamed. "We've always thought so. I also had a large vegetable garden there, but I just can't seem to work like I used to. Kathie does most of the work for me here."

"I don't see why you should have to work hard at this stage of your life," Tess said, instinctively responding to the touch of sadness she heard in the older woman's voice. "After all, your retirement years are to enjoy."

Alma abruptly stopped and looked at her. "But you see, it's never been work for me. Taking care of my family and making gardens for them to both appreciate and to eat from has always been a joy for me. Someday, when you have your own family, you'll understand."

Tess couldn't think of a thing to say. She couldn't even begin to imagine herself with a family such as Alma was talking about, much less a garden to tend.

"Start with those roses there." Alma handed a pair of garden scissors to her. "You're a very sweet girl, Tess, but the truth is, Ben and I are past retirement. We're at the end of our lives, and we know it."

It was all the pictures, she supposed. She'd seen Alma and Ben from the beginning of their life together until now, which was nearly the end. But she found she really cared for this woman and her husband. Once again, she rushed to reassure her. "You don't know that for sure. None of us knows what's going to happen tomorrow." She bent to cut several white roses, then straightened to place them in the basket Alma carried.

This time Alma didn't bother correcting her. "I'm so glad we've had this opportunity to meet you, Tess. I always knew it would take an extraordinary girl to make Nick give up his wandering ways, and I can tell right off that you are that girl."

She shook her head, unwilling in this instance to let Alma get her hopes raised. "You may be reading too much into our, uh, relationship. Nick and I have really only just met." Then again, time, in the normal sense, didn't seem to apply to them.

"Nonsense. I know my Nick." She pointed to a grouping of irises. "Take some of those. Particularly the purple ones. They're very special. I brought cuttings of them from our home. They're from the original bunch that my mother-in-law started years ago."

"Really? I saw them this morning, and they're still beautiful."

Alma nodded. "It's a good feeling to know that they've survived through the generations. Kathie has them at her house, too. And before you leave, I'm going to have Nick shovel you a start of them. It will make me feel good to know that they'll be passing into your hands, so that your children and your grandchildren will be able to enjoy them as much as the previous generations."

"Thank you. That's very kind of you." A multitude of emotions nearly overwhelmed Tess. To her surprise, she was close to breaking into tears. But she couldn't allow herself to show any of what she was feeling. She didn't want to distress Alma in any way.

Obviously Alma thought she and Nick would be getting married and establishing their own home, and Tess couldn't find it in her heart to tell her that she was wrong. More than likely she would find out soon enough.

"Over there." Once again Alma pointed, this time to a grouping of creamy yellow flowers. "Those are spring bells. They'll look nice in your bouquet."

Nodding compliantly, Tess cut several stalks of the delicate-looking flower.

"Have you had a chance yet to see much of the land around our home?"

"Only a little."

"When you go back, look around if you can. When Nick was a little boy, he learned every inch of those cliffs, hills and arroyos. And not just ours. He'd explore our neighbors' land as well. Fences of any kind never much bothered him. Cut yourself a few snapdragons, too."

"Okay, but this is the last. Your basket is full, and what I've already cut will give me a beautiful bouquet."

Even though Alma was looking right at her, Tess wasn't sure she'd heard what she'd said.

"It seems to me that Nick has been searching for something his entire life. He's always been a restless, serious boy. When he was young, he'd go off on his own for hours at a time. By late afternoon, I'd always start to worry about him, but along about sundown, here he'd come, his pockets and hands filled with the treasure he'd found." Alma smiled. "Rocks, mostly, but he'd stick them in his pockets because he thought they were pretty, or shiny, or had a nice shape. I had big baskets of his rocks everywhere, but I never dared throw one of them out. Eventually I got the idea of placing them in prominent places in my garden, which made him happy. And I can't tell you how many arrow heads he found, plus agates of Apache tears, tiger's eyes and snowflakes. He had boxes of each of them.''

Lost in reverie, Alma smiled. "Then, as he grew older, his interests changed, but he was as restless and solemn as he'd been as a boy. Sports and girls became important to him, but they didn't satisfy him. Every chance he got, he'd go out walking, still searching for something, still looking for treasure, I suppose. Our son never cared one way or the other about the *Águila* or its treasure, but Nick…that boy was born with his grandpa's dreams in his soul.''

"Then he should be happy now, because he's found the treasure.''

Slowly Alma focused on her. "Yes, he's found the *Águila*'s treasure, but he's more restless than I've ever seen him—oh, not on the outside, but on the inside. He tries to hide it from us, but I know him too well. Before Ben dies, Nick wants more than anything in the world to be able to give his grandpa his life's dream. He wants to stack that gold in the middle of town so that everyone will know how wrong they were about his grandpa and his great-grandpa. In a way, it's a passion he shares with Ben, except with Ben, the passion goes deeper. He's the one who had to watch helplessly as his papa was constantly humiliated and eventually became a broken man. And Ben's the one who was made to suffer so by other kids. I firmly believe that showing people the proof of that gold is what's keeping Ben alive.''

Alma took Tess's breath away. She'd never met any woman like her. "And do you think if Nick is able to do that for his grandfather that Nick will at last be satisfied and his restlessness will finally go away?''

"I think the answer to your question lies in you.''

"Me?'' she asked, surprised.

"Nick is in love with you, child. Nothing could be plainer to me. But what's not plain is whether you love him in return. I hope you do. Nick's trying so hard to please his grandpa, but I don't want *his* dreams to get lost in the process."

"His dreams?"

"Why, child, ultimately what everyone wants is a deep and abiding love, now isn't it?"

She was at a loss for words. Alma's life was so different than hers. The way in which she'd been brought up had left little time for dreaming.

Alma glanced around her garden. "We should go inside now. I'll wrap the flowers for you so they'll stay nice and fresh until you can get them in water."

"Thank you." What else could she say? She couldn't reassure Alma about any of the things that were concerning her. She couldn't tell her that she would stop drilling. She couldn't tell her love was going to smooth the rocky path she and Nick were on, because there was no love. And for them, at the end, there would be no happily-ever-after love story. Nick had a restless soul that more than likely could never be soothed by love. As for her, she had never even been taught *how* to love.

While Nick straightened the house in preparation for leaving, Tess placed a call to Ron and asked that he meet her at the airport with an overnight bag and a briefcase filled with work. She also asked that he charter a plane and have it ready to go when she landed.

The flight to Corpus Christi was relatively silent. As soon as the plane taxied to a stop, Tess was out of her seat and heading toward the cabin door.

"Wait, Tess."

"I'll wait by the bottom of the stairs."

She opened the door, then reached for her bouquet of flowers and the brown paper bag that held her start of irises. At the bottom of the stairs, she found Ron. "Were you able to do everything I asked?"

Ron nodded. "The plane's close. Everything you requested is already on board, including the pilot."

"Excellent. Thank you."

"No problem. Listen, Tess. I'm so sorry I didn't get your message last night. I was—"

"Never mind. It's over, and I'm sure I'll never find myself in that situation again. But just in case, make sure that the next time you spend the night away from home, you call in for messages."

"Don't worry. I've learned my lesson."

"Good. Will you please take these flowers to the house and put them in a vase for me?" She thought for a second. "Then put them in my bedroom. I'll be back tomorrow." She handed the flowers and the paper bag to him. "Put the irises in the pantry for now. We'll plant them in a pot tomorrow."

"Sure. Oh, there's just one thing he said to tell you."

"What's that?"

"He said he may not be able to stay awake until you get there."

She nodded. "I understand."

Nick came down the stairs. He saw Ron, then cut his gaze to her. "Why is he here?"

"Ron, can you give me a minute?"

"Certainly. I'll be waiting by the terminal door."

Tess waited until her assistant was out of earshot. "Ron is here because I asked him to be." She paused, trying to decide what she wanted to say. In many ways she felt as disoriented as if she'd just returned from another planet where warm, loving families were the norm. On her planet, the only thing that counted was lots of big, healthy numbers that represented millions and millions of dollars.

She tilted her head and looked at him. "Why did you tell your grandparents that I might stop the drilling?"

"Because under the circumstances they wouldn't have understood a flat no. This way, if you say no, they'll think you did your best."

"Would the truth be so hard for them to understand?" Even as she asked the question, she knew the answer because she'd met them, seen their life through pictures, seen Alma's garden and been given a start of her cherished irises. "You know, Nick, it all basically boils down to one thing. You're asking me to give up millions so that you can make millions. What's so hard to understand about that?" Once again, she knew the answer. The *Águila*'s gold didn't represent money to Ben and Alma. It represented vindication.

He regarded her calmly. "You sound upset."

She laughed. "Yeah, as a matter of fact I am. By introducing me to your grandparents, you once again attempted to stack the deck in your favor."

"Did it work?"

She closed her eyes for a moment. Without knowing it, he'd put her in an untenable position. If she did what was best for him and his grandparents, it would put her in a far more desperate position than she was in now. In fact, it would end a large part of her life that was as vital to her as air.

On the other hand, if she did what was best for her, it would be the end of the light and hope in Nick's grandfather's eyes, which for Nick, would be unforgivable. Not only that, it would crush him, his grandfather and his grandmother, and no doubt bring an early death to his grandfather. Plus, she would never see Nick again.

She opened her eyes. "I'll try."

"What does that mean?"

"It means I'm going to try to see if there's a way I can stop drilling for the period of time you want, but at this moment I can't give you any promises."

Frustration etched lines into his face. "But whether to drill or not is up to you, right?"

"Ultimately, yes. Whether I proceed or not will be my decision. But...I need additional information, and there's only one person who can give it to me. Then and only then will I be able to give you an answer that might be different than the one I've already given you."

He shook his head. "I still don't understand."

"How could you?" She smiled slightly. "Whichever way my decision goes, I'll call you when I get back tomorrow."

He caught her arm before she could walk away. "What do you mean, when you get back? Where are you going?"

"I told you. There's someone I need to talk to, and to do that, the best way is to go to him."

"Then I'll go, too."

"No way, no how. I have to go alone."

He stared at her, no doubt trying to read her, but in this part of the game of life, she'd been schooled by the best.

"Why?" he finally asked.

She smiled, in complete sympathy with his inability to understand. "Just because you successfully kidnapped me for almost twenty-four hours doesn't mean you now have the right to butt into my life and know all my comings and goings."

Slowly he released her arm. "No, I guess I don't. You said you'd call me, right?"

She nodded. "As soon as I get back into town."

He exhaled a long breath. "And would it be too much to ask when you think that will be?"

"Sometime tomorrow afternoon or evening."

"Okay, then, I'll be waiting."

# Seven

The sun was rising, streaking the sky with corals and pinks. Wrapped in a blanket and sipping a cup of coffee, Tess rocked in one of the many rocking chairs that had lined Uncle William's front porch since her earliest remembrance. The house where she and her sisters had been raised sat less than a mile from Uncle William's, but Kit was the only one who lived there now.

When her father and his brother, William, had first come to this land west of Dallas and Fort Worth that would become the Double B Ranch, they'd each built a home. Uncle William's was a large, rambling two-story house with a long, wide front porch and rooms that no one had ever used.

Her father had built an equally large two-story house, but there was nothing rambling about it. Its lines were clean and precise, with no wasted space and a definite purpose for each room. Besides his bedroom, he'd built exactly three extra bedrooms, rooms he'd expected her mother to fill with his sons. Instead she'd presented him with three daughters in as many years, and then had had the bad luck to die in a car accident on the way back from a shopping trip to Dallas.

Tess took another sip of coffee and pondered the ways of her family. If she'd chosen, she could have spent the night in the house and in the bedroom she'd grown up in. She might even have had a chance to visit with Kit. But the bedroom held no fond memories for her, and to visit with Kit, she would have to catch her first. Kit was perpetual motion.

In the end, she'd had the ranch hand who had picked her up last night from the landing strip bring her here to Uncle William's. After all, he was the one she was here to see, and as soon as she did, she had to fly to Corpus. As for the pilot, he had been taken to the comfortable guest house, built to look like the equally comfortable bunkhouses where the ranch hands lived. His close proximity insured there would be no delay when she was ready to leave.

Ellie stuck her lined face around the screen door. "There you are, child. I'd thought you might want to sleep in a bit, but I should've known better. None of you girls ever slept past sunup."

Tess smiled dryly. "That's because our father wouldn't let us."

"Well, his lesson took real good." Ellie closed the screen door behind her, ambled to the rocking chair beside hers and settled her large, big-boned frame into it. "Many's the dawn I look out my bedroom window and see that sister of yours streaking past the house on that big devil of a stallion she rides, that red hair of hers streaming out behind her like a flag."

Tess nodded. "No one else can ride him but Kit."

"You mean no one *wants* to ride him but her. Oowee, that devil scares me."

Tess grinned with affection. "Well, if that's the case, he's the only thing I've ever known you to be afraid of."

Back in the forties, Ellie had come to the Double B as a young girl, ready and willing to tackle anything, including the duties of a ranch hand. But Uncle William, a bachelor then, hadn't thought riding fences and herding cattle was fit work for a young girl, so much to Ellie's disappointment, he'd made her his housekeeper. But not even he had able to keep Ellie inside all the time.

Uncle William had always said he'd never known a woman who could come up with as many excuses for being outside as she could. And so slowly the sun and the years had changed her appearance. Her skin was wrinkled and leathery, her hair gray, her shoulders stooped, but her strength, will and commonsense approach to life remained the same.

Ellie had outlived Tess's father and mother, along with Uncle William's wife. Now it looked as if Ellie would outlive Uncle William, too.

"You sure know how to make good coffee, Miss Tess, but you're 'bout the only one of your family who does. Miss Kit can't be bothered, and Miss Jill prefers tea. Now where do you suppose she got that from?"

Tess laughed. "I don't have a clue." When she and her sisters were born, Ellie had affixed the Miss to their name, and, despite their protests as they'd grown older, she'd made it clear that she considered Miss to be a part of their names. "We didn't have too much time to talk last night. How is Uncle William doing?"

"'Bout the same. Like all of us, he has his good days and his bad. I'll tell you one thing, he sure was sorry to miss your party."

"If he wasn't feeling well, he did the right thing by staying home."

Ellie shook her head. "He don't like to hear this, but just between me, you and the fence post, I think his travelin' days are over."

"I don't like to hear that, either. In fact, I don't even want to think about what that means." Uncle William was the glue that held her family, such as it was, together. As independent as she and her sisters were, they each, in their own way, relied on him. She glanced at her watch. "When does he usually get up?"

"It all depends on the kind of night he has, but soon now he'll be wakin' up, and Wilbur will be wanderin' over. Directly, I'll be goin' in and startin' breakfast. Wilbur'll get your uncle up, washed and dressed. Then he'll be ready to see you."

"Good." Wilbur was about a decade younger than her uncle, but he'd worked on the Double B from the beginning and was one of the two men in the world her uncle would allow to help him. Des was the other.

"Why don't you come on in with me and you can catch me up on your news, especially that party of yours. I saw Miss Kit on her way to the airstrip wearing nothin' but jeans and a T-shirt. I told her she needed to wear somethin' a bit nicer, but she just laughed and went on her way with Rodney, that new hand of ours."

Tess nodded. "Kit doesn't worry about the rules, written or otherwise—we all know that."

Ellie rolled her eyes. "Lord, yes, we *do* know that."

"But Kit looked fine, and I think she and Rodney had a good time."

The older woman snorted with disdain. "That Rodney is another one of those boys caught up in what he thinks is the glamour of being a cowboy. Me 'n' Wilbur got a bet

going. He thinks the boy'll last another month, mainly
'cause he fancies Miss Kit so much. Me, I don't think he'll
make it another week.'' Ellie grinned. ''You come on in
now, you hear?''

''In a few minutes, when I finish my coffee.''

As soon as she was alone again, Tess returned her gaze
to the horizon. The sun had risen above it, a brilliant,
golden ball full of promise for a new day. And staring at
the sun, she knew without a doubt that Nick was also
awake.

''Morning, Tess,'' Wilbur said, wheeling her uncle into
the big front room where the morning sun flooded.

Several years ago, when Uncle William had realized he
was losing his mobility, he'd moved back to the ranch from
Dallas and ordered his large desk to be relocated to this
room. He'd also had large picture windows installed along
each wall to bring as much of the ranch as was possible
indoors. Here he could continue overseeing his businesses
and, at the same time, have the best possible views of his
beloved ranch.

''Good morning, Wilbur. Good morning, Uncle William.''

Wilbur wheeled her uncle to his desk. Then, with a nod
and a smile to Tess, he left.

''I'm so happy to see you, Tess. When I couldn't make
your party, I was afraid it would be a while before I'd be
able to see you again.''

Tess circled the desk to kiss her uncle. ''I missed you,
but I completely understood why you couldn't come.''

''Well, then, you're one up on me,'' he grumbled, ''because I didn't understand it at all. It was that damn doctor
of mine. If I didn't have such a good time arguing with
him, I'd get another doctor.'' He paused while Ellie came

in with a saucer full of prescription medicine and vitamins, along with a large glass of orange juice. When she left, he drank a little of the orange juice and pointedly ignored the contents of the saucer. "I don't suppose that son of mine showed up, either, did he?" Des had been a young boy when his mother had married Uncle William, and from the beginning, Uncle William had never called him anything but son.

"No, no, he didn't." Tess pulled a chair to the side of the desk. "How are you?" she asked, searching his face for signs of decline that hadn't been there the last time she'd seen him. Happily, she found none.

"I'm fine, I'm fine, and don't you believe otherwise. I'm going to outlive that doctor of mine just so I can prove his prognostications of doom and gloom wrong."

She laughed with delight. In that moment, she truly believed her uncle would live forever. In that moment, he seemed the same as he'd always been, a big man with a booming voice, enormous strength and a brilliant mind. Her father had been born with the very same characteristics. Together, the two of them had carved a great ranch out of a hostile land and built a multimillion-dollar corporation that today was respected all over the world. Unfortunately, though, unlike her uncle, there had been no place in her father for affection, laughter and humor. "You just don't know how happy that makes me."

He reached over and took her hand. His skin felt dry, but the strength she'd always known remained. "You, your sisters and Des are what keep me going. You still need me, and as long as that continues, I'll be here for you."

Tess blinked back tears. "Thank you, but you should know, there'll never come a day when we won't need you."

He laughed. "That's music to an old man's ears, even if

I know it's not the truth. But at any rate, let's get down to the reason you're here. Is it something to do with your well? Or is it something to do with the man Des told me had kidnapped you off to Uvalde?''

She grimaced. She wished Des hadn't put it quite that way, no matter how accurate he'd been. "It's about both, actually. And also about my father's will.''

He released her hand and sat back in his wheelchair. "Tell me about it.''

She did. She told him about the well, how she felt it had the potential to be the greatest moneymaker of all her sites yet that there was no way she could know that for certain until the drill actually hit oil and they began pumping. Then she told him about Nick, his family and its history, and about the hope of his grandfather to use the treasure for vindication.

She saved the conflict between Nick and herself for last. She reported the precarious position of the ship and how one slight miscalculation on her rig could send the ship and its treasure over the scarp where it would lie buried for years, maybe for all time. Last, she explained about Ben's health and Nick's plea that she halt the drilling for at least three months.

When she fell silent, her uncle let out a long breath. "Well, I can certainly see your problem. I also see something else. You're in love with this Nick Trejo.''

She opened her mouth to tell him he was wrong, then closed it. Unbidden, images and emotions flashed through her head and heart, one after the other—the way he could make her go weak at the knees with just a smile, the way he'd made her want him last night in the living room of the farmhouse, the way she'd turned down Des's help, when just twenty-four hours earlier, she would have gone to any lengths to gain his attention.

God, why hadn't she seen it before? The knowledge had been right there in front of her the whole time, but she'd kept pushing it to the back of her mind. Now, though, she had no choice but to face it. She *did* love Nick.

Slowly she nodded. "Yes, I'm afraid I do. But unless I can figure out a way to give him what he wants, he'll never love me in return."

Uncle William's gray eyebrows shot straight up. "If his love is dependent on your granting him what he wants, then his love isn't worth having."

She knew he was right. She also regretted stating it the way she had. "Perhaps it would be more accurate to say that no matter which way things go, I doubt if he'll ever love me."

"Okay, then, in that case it sounds as if he's going after you for two reasons. Because you're a smart, beautiful woman and he just plain wants you, and because—"

"I never said—"

"You didn't have to. He wants you physically, and he wants you to cease drilling for a spell. But then you already know those two things. What do you want from me?" Her uncle was nothing if not earthy and direct.

"I want to talk to you about my father's will and the clause that states that unless I've earned *his* idea of a fortune within ten years of his death, I'll lose my portion of the company." She folded her arms across her waist, comforting herself, in a way. "And you know as well as I do that for most people the figure our father gave me and my sisters would be impossible to attain."

"But from what you've said, this well is going to put you over the top, though with very little time to spare."

She nodded. "Uncle William, I'm betting everything I've got on just that. Still, it'll take months before I know for sure."

Uncle William regarded her gravely. "And you only have a little under ten months left to do it."

"Right, but it's doable." She sat forward, the excitement she felt for the new well seeping into her voice and expression. "If I'm lucky, we'll hit oil in two more months, give or take a couple of weeks. Then I'll have eight months to pump enough oil to give me the figures I need. But that's if I have no major holdups or breakdowns and, at the same time, drill twenty-four hours a day, seven days a week. The problem is, I understand and sympathize with what Nick is trying to do. I'd love to be able to shut down and give him whatever time he needs."

She rose and began to pace. "So what I'm hoping for from you is a way to interpret my father's will in a different manner, but that would still keep it within its legal boundaries. For instance, if I strike oil but the well hasn't yet produced enough, could I slip under my father's guidelines on the grounds that there is the potential for the amount named?"

He sighed. "I wish I could tell you yes, honey, but your father's will couldn't have been more clear. He saw to that. We made up our wills together, you know, and when he told me about that clause, I counseled him against it. I just didn't feel he was being fair to you girls, but your father was insistent. He saw it as a way to make the three of you prove you were worthy of inheriting your shares of the company."

Tess dropped her head, trying to hide the tears she couldn't seem to keep back. "To prove we were *worthy*. For any other man, love of his children would be enough." She walked to one of the windows and blindly gazed out. "He controlled us in life, and now he's controlling us in death. Most children look forward to their birthdays, but all they meant to us was more responsibilities, more challenges, more goals to be met. He kept raising the proverbial bar.''

''Yeah, I know.'' Regret laced her uncle's voice. ''I've never known a man who wanted sons as badly as he did. But when you girls came along instead, he decided it was his job to make you tough.''

''And don't forget the competitive part. Today, Kit, Jill and I will go to practically any lengths to one up each other.''

''I know, honey.''

''And while he was alive, we'd work until we were exhausted, trying to please him, yet when we accomplished what he asked of us, he barely acknowledged our achievement. It was almost like he wanted us to fail.'' She looked at her uncle. ''Did he?''

Reluctance shaded his tone. ''Maybe in some twisted way he wanted to prove that he was right in thinking sons would have been superior to daughters.''

''I don't know about Kit and Jill, but I've worked my entire life to prove him wrong.''

He sighed heavily. ''I can't count the number of times he and I fought over the way he treated the three of you. I called him every name in the book, but when it came to you girls, he ignored me.''

She walked slowly to the desk. ''More than once I've actually wondered if Mother's death was an accident.''

His head shot up, and his eyes sharpened. ''What do you mean?''

''Knowing Father, I can only imagine the hell he made her life because he'd expected her to produce sons and instead she'd given him daughters. Maybe she decided... Who knows.''

He didn't say a thing. He didn't have to. She walked around his desk and sat down. ''Tell me something, Uncle

William. You knew him better than anyone else in the world. Do you honestly think he ever loved us?''

He took several moments to ponder her question. ''It's hard to say for certain, but in his own way, yes, I think so. If he didn't, he would have left you alone and wouldn't have cared what you did.''

''What an awful way to love.'' She wiped the tears from her eyes. ''Jill's already proved herself worthy of her one-sixth of the company. She's already hit the mark and made even more, despite the fact that she has another year, because she's a year younger than I am. Kit has two more years.''

''Jill has already reached her mark because real estate is a booming market.'' He watched her for a moment. ''I wish I could help you with this, but, again, the will is very clear. You have to make the money yourself. No gifts.''

''I know.''

''So what are you going to do?''

Her lips firmed. ''I don't have a choice.''

''That's not entirely true, you know. Even if you lost your one-sixth of the company, you'd still be able to run your division.''

''Right,'' she said flatly. ''And I'd be nothing more than a hired employee. Besides you and Des, I'd have to answer to Jill and Kit. They'd have the right to examine every decision I made, and to say yes or no to any undertaking I might want to pursue. And that would be completely intolerable to me.'' Not only that, she reflected with pain. If she couldn't make the money by her deadline, her father would win. That was also intolerable to her. She shook her head. ''No, thanks to Father, I really have only one way to go. My part of Baron International is *my* legacy, *my* right. It would destroy me to lose my part of the family business, and I'm going to do whatever I have to do to keep it.''

# Eight

Tess wandered to the open French doors that led from her bedroom to the terrace. Against a black sky, dark gray clouds piled up over the Gulf, one atop the other.

Lightning streaked the horizon. Thunder rolled in the distance. The wind strengthened by the minute. A storm was brewing, and the turbulent atmosphere suited her dark, restless mood.

*Nick.* Where was he tonight? She hoped he had been able to secure the *Águila* as much as was possible. But more than that, she prayed he was safely on land. According to reports, the major portion of the storm looked as if it would stay far out at sea, and Corpus and its surrounding areas would only get grazed by its edge. Still, it would be foolish not to take precautions.

If she had called Nick, as she'd promised she would when she returned from the Double B, she might know where he was. But she was a bona fide, freely admitted coward and was trying to put off as long as possible the moment when she would have to say no to him for the final time.

Sipping at a glass of burgundy wine, she leaned against the door and lifted her face to the mist-filled wind. Even though she'd worked at her usual frenetic pace all afternoon, her mind had been on the conversation she'd had with Uncle William and the irrefutable fact that, as they talked, had hit her squarely between her eyes.

*She loved Nick.*

The idea astounded her. She didn't even know *how* to love, perhaps because, to her knowledge, she'd never been truly loved. Yet there was no doubt. She was definitely in love with Nick.

Right from the first, the signs had been there, all of them in big, bright, red neon letters. How could she have missed them?

There was the way he'd mesmerized her on the night of her birthday and the way her body had melted against his when they'd danced. There was the way she'd so easily acquiesced to the idea of flying to some unknown destination for dinner and the stunning fact that she'd turned down Des's offer for help.

But in her defense, she'd never been in love before. She'd never even experienced what she would consider normal love—the love of a child for a parent or vice versa, or even the love of one sister for another. No wonder she hadn't recognized the signs.

Drops of rain began to fall, splattering the terrace. The lightweight ivory caftan she'd changed into after work was getting wet. She didn't care.

The rain was cool. Her skin was hot. She wanted Nick.

She wanted to see him, to touch him, to make love to him as they almost had the night before last. And she

wanted him to hold her and kiss her until they both forgot
that their lives were going in two different directions and
that they could never have a future together.

She might not know anything about love, but she was
learning fast. Love hurt, and there wasn't a thing she could
do about it.

She couldn't pursue Nick, nor could she tell him of her
love. But for the rest of her life he would remain in her
heart, a heart that was already breaking. Somehow, in some
way, she was going to have to learn how to bear it.

The agony of it was that Nick had come along at literally
the most critical time of her life. If things had been different
in their lives, if they'd met under any other circumstances,
where neither of them wanted anything from the other except truth and trust, they might have had a chance.

Damn her father!

She let out a long breath. She should have called Nick
this afternoon, as she'd promised. She was only prolonging
the inevitable. This afternoon, this evening, tomorrow, a
month from now, her answer would still have to be the
same. She should get it over with, but she couldn't make
herself. She needed this time, this respite, when she could
tell herself that Nick didn't hate her. Not yet, at any rate.

The rain was coming down heavier, and still she wasn't
ready to go in. She was hurting too much, wanting too
much. Lightning split the sky. A boom of thunder shook
the windowpanes of the door she leaned against. Lightning
again charged the air with electricity.

Nick walked out of the dark rain. Water streamed off his
hair, his face, his forearms. His clothing was soaked and
plastered to his hard body. He stopped several feet from
her, his hands balled into fists at his sides, his stance wide
and firm. Anger and heat filled his gaze as it raked her from
the top of her head right down to her bare feet. At that

instant he seemed a part of the storm—fierce, elemental, dangerous.

"You didn't call."

Unable to take her gaze off him, she slowly shook her head. "It was a hectic day and I... " There wasn't a single thing she could say that would assuage his wrath.

"Damn you, Tess." His deep voice rolled over her like thunder. "You *had* to know I was waiting."

"I'm so sorry—"

"Your answer is no, isn't it? *Isn't* it? And *that's* why you didn't call."

"Nick, I tried—"

"Damn you." Slowly he started toward her. "Damn me. *Damn* our situation." As he reached her, he extended his hand past her head to brace himself against the door. "And the worst part of it is that right now, I don't care."

She didn't either. Nothing mattered except the craving for him that involved every part of her. Tomorrow she would care. But not tonight.

He sank his body against hers until he had her pressed back against the door. Then he crushed his mouth on hers and thrust his tongue deep into her mouth.

*This night, this lovemaking, was meant to be.* The vague thought whispered loudly in her mind. Over the past few days, their sexual need for each other had gathered momentum until this moment when neither of them could do anything to stop it.

When he'd walked out of the storm, she'd taken one look at him and known it didn't matter whether or not he would try to use sex as a way of getting what he wanted. She wanted him, and this one night she would have him.

She let go of any restrictions, constraints or reserves and pushed away any and all doubts. She stood on tiptoes, slipped her arms around his neck and returned his kiss with all the enthusiasm and love she possessed.

It didn't matter that he didn't love her. She loved him, and for tonight that would be enough.

The fury of the storm continued, the rain soaking her hair and skin. But the fire inside her kept growing, astounding her, taking her over until she was all heat and need. He kissed her lips, her face, her neck, seemingly drinking in the rain and the taste of her, and she did the same to him, licking his neck and face. She was starving for him.

His hand grasped her breast; then, leaning down, he drew the nipple and the wet, transparent caftan that covered it into his mouth and strongly sucked. Her head fell back, her womb contracted, and softly she moaned. She was helpless against the onslaught of heated sensations that followed one after the other. And just when she thought she'd reached the pinnacle of the amount of pleasure she could feel, he showed her she was wrong by turning his attention to her other breast, pulling that nipple into his mouth, briefly releasing it, then tugging at it again and again until she was almost crazed with desire.

Fire coiled through her to the point that she no longer felt the cool rain against her skin. In fact, she felt so hot that she was surprised the rain didn't dry as soon as it landed on her skin.

"Nobody stops," she whispered, sliding her fingers through his hair, then down to the buttons of his shirt. She began to undo them.

He lifted his head from her breast and stared at her with a brilliant heat. "Nobody stops," he muttered, then kissed her once more with an urgency that matched hers.

He dropped his hands to the caftan at her thighs and gathered the wet cloth. Wrenching his mouth from hers, he pulled the caftan up and over her head and tossed it onto the rain-drenched terrace. Then he crushed his mouth down on hers with a desperation she felt to her bones.

She could no longer tell the loud beat of her heart from the booming thunder. She could no longer tell whether the world was spinning around her or whether Nick was making her feel as if it was. She pushed the edges of his shirt aside and immediately closed her mouth over one of his rigid nipples.

With a loud groan he plowed his fingers through her hair and held her head against him. Fascinated, enthralled, she lightly bit and nibbled his nipple, then circled it with her tongue, lapping up the rain and him. She'd never known a man's nipple could be so erotic.

Without warning, he knelt before her. His hands gripped her bare buttocks, caressing them, and his tongue dipped into her navel, where again he drank from her. Then slowly, hotly, his mouth slid downward.

She was glad for the support of the door. Her legs felt weak. Her breathing became labored. Her chest hurt. And a wonderful, unbearable ache built between her legs.

Acting on pure, inexplicable instinct, she shifted her stance and parted her legs. She'd had sex a couple of times—infinitely forgettable sex. Still, she would have thought she was prepared for anything regarding sex. She wasn't. Not at all.

His fingers opened the two folds that guarded that most intimate part of her; then his tongue thrust against the achingly sensitive nub. Like a bolt of lightning, pleasure shocked through her, and she cried out. "Oh, Nick!"

The wind and rain absorbed her words as his tongue stroked and licked. Her fingers tightened in his hair. She climaxed—hard, fast and powerful.

Aftershocks shuddered through her as her body absorbed the sweet, hot ecstasy. But before she had a chance to catch

her breath, he straightened and lifted her. She wrapped her
legs around him and wound her arms around his neck. As
she had been at the farm house, she was open against the
denim of his jeans and his hard sex.

He walked with her into the bedroom. Impossibly, she
climaxed again. Crying out, she held on to him as if he
were life itself. And indeed, at that moment, he *was* her
entire life, her entire world.

On her bed, she could hardly bear the wait for him. Lying
on her back, she drew up her knees, agonizingly sensitized.
A bedside lamp illuminated the room, along with the occasional flash of lightning. She tried to concentrate on
breathing as she watched Nick strip out of his clothes, but
she wasn't certain she always breathed.

He was magnificent. Lean muscles shifted and rippled
beneath his bronze skin as he undressed. Scars appeared
that she hadn't had a chance to see before, but now she
longed to touch them. Fine black hair covered his chest and
arrowed down to his groin, where his sex throbbed with
power. He was a picture of pure, undiluted virile masculinity.

A new wave of desire quivered through her. As if he
could feel what she felt, his amber gaze cut to her and
scorched her skin.

She couldn't think of a thing to say. Besides, in the short
time they'd known each other, they'd already said so much.
For tonight, at least, maybe words weren't necessary. Tonight was the time to let their bodies speak, and what they
were speaking of was basic needs and elemental passion.
They were speaking *truths,* truths that the two of them
would never verbally speak of to each other.

He came to her and positioned himself over her. His
breathing was rough, his body taut, his face tight with intensity. She expected him to immediately enter her, wanted,

needed him to. Yet instead he stared at her. Feverishly, fleetingly, she wondered what he was thinking, but she wanted him too badly to spend time asking him or trying to figure it out.

This night would never come again, and as surely as the sun would rise tomorrow, discord would insert itself between them. For now, for tonight, she wanted there to be only pleasure between them—pure, white-hot, ecstatic pleasure.

Later, she supposed, she would be shocked at her attitude and behavior. It was so radically different from who and what she was normally. Or maybe, deep down, tonight, she *was* the person she was supposed to be, and she'd only needed the right man to make her understand that.

Except Nick was the wrong man.

Determinedly she smiled up at him, slid her hands to his shoulders, then to his back. They were both slick with rain. "Nick," she whispered, pleading. "Please. Oh, *please.*"

With his jaw clenched, he drew back his hips and drove deeply into her, burying himself completely in her. A hard shudder racked his body, a shudder that she felt deep inside her and that nearly brought her to climax again. With a soft moan, she wrapped her arms and legs around him and held him to her as tightly as she could. She didn't think she'd ever felt anything as wonderful as having him inside her. It was insanity. It was bone-deep rapture and satisfaction.

She was going to peak again soon. She could feel it. She was almost there. She wanted it to happen immediately, and at the same time, she wanted to prolong as much as possible the pleasure of having Nick inside her. But she wasn't in charge.

He hammered in and out of her like a man out of control, and mindlessly she matched his rhythm, lifting and undulating her hips, attempting to take him deeper and deeper into her.

Then it started again. Fire and passion built, filling her, taking her over. Her fingers clutched his shoulders. She opened her eyes and looked at Nick. His face was strained, his neck muscles corded, the muscles of his back and shoulders bunched, but in his eyes she saw the sure knowledge that he knew exactly what she was feeling and that he was with her.

He reached for one of her hands and tightly entwined their fingers. As a harsh sound tore out of him, he drove into her with short, quick strokes. They strained together, urgent, frantic, almost mad with the sweet agony of pleasure. Then he thrust deeply into her, once, twice, three times.

Then it happened. She arched her back as she climaxed, and a flaming ecstasy took her soaring up and over an unknown precipice. At the same time, Nick convulsed with his own completion. And as he had promised her with his hot amber gaze, this time they soared together.

A soft rain fell on the terrace. The only other sound Tess could hear was Nick's uneven breathing as he lay beside her. Inches separated them, though it felt like miles.

He wasn't asleep. Though he lay perfectly still, she could feel the energy and heat that radiated off his body. Somehow, though, she knew that this time the heat and energy didn't come from sexual desire. She'd known that feeling, and this was different. This feeling came from anger. Anger at her, no doubt, for telling him no. Anger at himself for giving in to his desire for a woman who wouldn't give him what he wanted.

Sadness overwhelmed her. She shivered and reached down to pull the sheet over her. Their passion had been spent. Now there was nothing between them, only a void that couldn't be filled.

She'd known this time would come, when Nick would feel nothing for her but disdain. But knowing it didn't make it any easier for her to deal with. She just wished he would say something. Anything would be better than this silence.

"I guess I should have closed the doors," she said softly. "The carpet must be soaked." She waited for some kind of response, and when it didn't come, she went on. "Not that it matters. If the damage is too bad, I'll have it replaced."

"Tell me something." His voice was equally soft, but the underlying hard tone she heard made her blood run cold. "When did you plan to give me the bad news?"

She looked at him. "Tomorrow. I was definitely going to call you tomorrow."

"You mean like you were definitely going to call me as soon as you returned from your mystery trip?"

There was nothing she could say to that. She'd already admitted to herself that she was being a coward when she'd made the decision to put off the call, though she had no intention of admitting it to him.

"No answer to that, Tess? Okay, then tell me something else."

She tensed. The sudden sharpness in his voice could have cut through steel. "What?"

"Did I ever have a chance?"

She quietly sighed. "I thought there might be a chance. I knew it was a long shot, but I checked it out anyway." She shook her head. "I tried, Nick. I really did."

He jammed a pillow behind his head. "Right."

"Look, there's no point in continuing to talk about this. I did try, but it didn't work out as I had hoped it might."

"What's to work out, Tess? It's easy. All you have to do is say stop."

"It's not that easy. It's much more involved than you'll ever know. In fact, nothing about any of this is easy."

He came up on one elbow and stared down at her. "Why not? You're the oil baron—or baroness, if you prefer—with money to burn. What's so difficult? You stop drilling for three months—hell, at this point I would take two. Then, after that time, you start up again. You can't be so cash poor that waiting a couple of months to bring up the oil will be that detrimental to your balance sheet."

She sat up, shoved the pillows into a pile behind her, then, taking the sheet with her, leaned against them. "You don't understand, Nick. You just don't."

He sat beside her, not bothering with the sheet. "Baby, have you ever got a way with understatement."

She shook her head—at his sarcasm, at the futility of this conversation, at her sadness. There was no way they would ever agree on this. In different ways, they were both hostages to the past. Neither could call the present their own.

"I'm waiting."

Her brow furrowed. "For what?"

"For an explanation."

"You and I have been over and over this subject, Nick. There's no point in continuing, because there's nothing more to be said. I'm not going to change my mind. I know that's hard for you to accept, but you're just going to have to."

"You're wrong. I *don't* have to accept it. Besides, maybe, just maybe, with enough talking and explaining, you and I can come to an agreement."

She would have smiled if she hadn't felt so much like crying. "You mean, you think with enough talking, I'll come around to your way of thinking."

"That's not what I said."

"No, but it's what you meant. Let's face it, Nick. No explanation, no matter how compelling, will matter to you. To your way of thinking, nothing is more important than getting that gold stacked in the middle of downtown Uvalde before your grandfather dies."

"You're right. You're absolutely right. But I'd just like to know, Tess. What reason do you have that could be more important than that?"

"Nothing that I could convince you of." The sheet was angled across his groin, leaving everything else bare. Shadows from the lamplight fell across his flat stomach and lower. Memories of the ecstasy they'd just shared came flooding back to her and her heart began to pound.

"Try." The word came out through bared teeth, and her mind snapped back to the subject at hand.

Her family had a tacit agreement that they never discussed their business with outsiders. However, in this case, if she'd thought it would do any good, she wouldn't have hesitated to tell him. But she knew it wouldn't help.

Nick would never be able to understand the deep-seated desire that had burned in her practically her whole life, the desire that went bone-marrow deep to prove to her father her worth. Using her father's own method of measurement, she desperately wanted to prove she was worthy of owning her part of his company. But most of all, she wanted to prove to him that she was worthy of his love and had been all along.

Of course she knew he would never know if and when she fulfilled his requirements. After all, he was dead. But *she* would know, and it would make all the difference in the world to her.

Upset, restless, she held the sheet to her with one hand and pleated its edges with the other. "As I said before, I can't convince you that I have a more compelling reason than you do. And to tell you the truth, you're probably right in thinking your reason is more important than mine.''

''Then why—''

''Because I *can't* stop the drilling, Nick. I just *can't,* and don't ask me again.'' She slipped off the bed, taking the sheet with her. Wrapping it around herself toga style, she crossed to the French doors. The moist air felt cool on her warm skin. Absently she reached up and ran her fingers through her hair in an attempt to put some order to it. Earlier, the rain had given it a thorough soaking, but during their lovemaking it had dried and she couldn't imagine how awful it must look. Not that it mattered. Nick would be leaving soon anyway.

She braced herself for what he would say next, but she heard nothing but the whisper of the gentle rain. She glanced at him over her shoulder. He was lying where she'd left him, obviously not at all self-conscious about his nakedness. Unfortunately she couldn't say the same. A look was all it took for her body to begin to ache and her mouth to water for just one more taste of him. Quickly she turned away. ''Aren't you going to say anything else?''

''No.''

Curious, she glanced over her shoulder again. ''Why?''

''You just told me to quit asking you to stop the drilling and that's exactly what I intend to do.''

''Just like that?''

''Just like that.''

She could hardly believe that he'd finally agreed to drop the subject. In a way she felt lighter, knowing there would be no more arguments. Except…without the conflict, there would also be no more reason for him to seek her out.

Her gaze returned to the rain-drenched patio. ''So what's

to become of the *Águila*? Do you think the storm did any damage to it?''

''I hope not. Despite all the fireworks, we really didn't get the brunt of the storm. I'll find out for sure tomorrow.''

She whirled. ''What do you mean? You're not going to dive again, are you?''

''Of course I am. I have to go where the ship is, and the ship is sitting on a scarp in relatively deep waters.''

Barely aware of what she was doing, she slowly walked toward him. ''But I've just told you I'm not going to stop drilling. That means it's way too dangerous for you or any of your men to continue to dive.''

''That's probably true.''

''Oh, it's definitely true. And knowing that, you're still going to do it?''

He fixed her with a level gaze. ''I don't have a choice, Tess. That gold is too important for Grandpa, and because of his health, I don't have a lot of time to waste.''

She sat on the edge of the bed. ''I know all that. You made sure I did. But as much as he wants it, would he want you to risk your life getting it?''

''Not if he knew.''

''But he must have some idea.''

''No, and that's the way it's going to stay.''

''Wait a minute. Remember, I met him. His mind is still sharp. If he really thinks about it for a minute, he'll figure it out.''

Nick shook his head. ''When he's pressed me for specifics, I've glossed over them and put heavy emphasis on the manned submersible.''

Her hand flew to her forehead. ''Of course. How could I have been so stupid? I'd forgotten about submersibles and their robotics capabilities. At the depth you're working, you'll use one, won't you?''

"Part of the time. I've managed to procure the use of a secondhand one, and it will certainly be of great help in bringing up the gold."

He moved off the bed and slipped into his briefs, then his jeans. Her heart sank. He was getting ready to leave.

"Part of the time?"

"A great deal of the *Águila* was made out of wood. Some of the wood is already gone. But I want to try to preserve what's left of the ship as best I can. And that means the work on the ship itself is too delicate to be left to anything robotic."

"The gold is what's important to you and your family. Why bother trying to preserve the ship?"

He gave her a half smile, but there was no humor in it. "I told you the other morning when we had breakfast out there." He nodded to the terrace. "I'm a professor of archaeology. Granted, the ship is not as old as some of the ships they've found and excavated on the east coast, but nevertheless, every nail and plank of the *Águila* is important to me."

"Nick, from what little I know about it, the current submersibles are very sophisticated. I've heard that robotics can give doctors the capability to operate on someone who's in a hospital miles away."

His eyebrows rose. "Does that sound like something you'd like done to you?"

"We're talking about a ship here, Nick. Not a human body."

"Everyone has to do things the way they feel is best." He sat on the bed and pulled on his socks and shoes.

She felt sick to her stomach. "It never occurred to me that you'd continue to dive."

"It's simple, Tess. We all do what we have to do. Just as you have to continue drilling, I have to continue diving."

He rose and made his way into the bathroom. He shut the door, but she could still hear water running and the flushing of the toilet.

When he came out, he looked freshly washed and much more dressed than she. She envied him both those things. He walked to the nightstand, where his watch lay. When had he taken it off?

She shifted on the bed so she could watch him. "Look, I know little or nothing about diving in the depths that you're talking about, but I do know that it's much more complicated and dangerous than scuba diving. I know you can't breathe simple oxygen. It's a mixture of something. And if the mixture is one little bit off, you're in trouble. Plus, if you come up too fast—"

His nod cut her off. "That's true." Casually he walked to the French doors, where she'd been minutes before.

"And I've heard of something called rapture—rapture of the deep."

"Nitrogen narcosis."

"Whatever. But I hear you get this feeling of great well-being, like being on really good drugs. Except you die, because it's almost certain you'll do something stupid, not to mention that the nitrogen pumping into your system is poisoning you."

He leaned an arm against the doorjamb. "Yeah, there's that."

"Damn it, Nick, are you *hearing* what I'm saying?"

Collected and composed, he turned to look at her. "Every single word."

She came off the bed. "And you know the dangers that can come from my rig. That's why you came to me in the first place."

His brows arched. "Your point?"

"My point, damn you, is that you've got no right to risk your life like that."

"It almost sounds as if you care."

She had to force herself to wait several beats before she answered. An instant reply would guarantee that she would give away her feelings for him. "Of course I care. I'd have the same concern for anyone I know."

He stood there, staring at her for what seemed an eternity. She could feel her pulse throb at the base of her neck and in the vein of her forehead. Had he guessed that she loved him?

"I'm sorry, Tess."

The anger and roughness in his voice had disappeared. Without warning, he had switched gears. "Sorry?"

He gestured to the bed. "I never meant for it to happen. I…" He rolled his shoulders.

She'd never seen him awkward, not in gesture or in word. But she was seeing it now.

He shook his head. "I tried my damnedest to resist you. Two nights ago, at the house, we almost—"

"I know." If she lived to be a hundred, she would probably never forget that moment when she'd made herself pull away from him.

"Just in case you have any doubts, stopping was one of the hardest things I've ever had to do in my life. And doing it took every ounce of control I had."

She shook her head. "It was hard for me, too, but I—"

"I know what you were thinking. You were afraid that I was using sex to get you to agree with what I wanted."

"I was thinking a lot of things."

"It's not true, Tess. It wasn't then, and it's not now."

"It doesn't matter what the reason was or is," she said almost wearily. "Let's face it, Nick. There have been too many emotions running between us. Sooner or later it was going to happen. And whether it happened two nights ago or tonight, it won't change my mind about the drilling."

"I know that. I've known that all along." He ran an unsteady hand through his sun-streaked dark hair. "The thing is, Tess, from the first, I wanted you almost too much. I still want you...way too much."

She could feel herself begin to tremble. "Is there such a thing as too much?"

"In our case, yeah, I think there just might be. Because if you take away the sex and leave only the subject of whether or not you'll stop drilling, there's no way both of us can win. Hell, we can't even compromise."

"I know." She looked at her hands. "But if it helps, I feel the same way...about wanting you too much."

"Yeah," he said softly, his eyes darkening with heat. "It helps."

Slowly he crossed to her. Automatically, naturally, she held out her arms to him. And as he took her back to bed, the sheet slowly slipped from her body.

When she awoke the next morning, she was alone.

# Nine

**R**on stuck his head around the door to her office. "Jill's on line two."

Tess almost groaned. She was already in a bad mood. She didn't need a call from her sister to make it worse. She swore if Jill murmured one patronizing or gloating word about the fact that she'd already met the will's requirements, she would hire a hit man to go after her. "Thanks, Ron." She picked up the phone.

"Good morning, Jill. To what do I owe this unexpected pleasure?" Her pleasant words didn't come close to matching her tone.

"I heard you were in danger."

Her mind went blank. "Danger?" She'd been too busy thinking about Nick and the night they'd spent together to consider much else.

"Oh, come on," Jill said impatiently. "Don't play

dumb. You got yourself kidnapped so that Des would feel like he needed to go rescue you.''

"Oh, yeah, that. Well, it wasn't exactly a kidnapping.''

"I heard it was.''

"I went willingly, but once I was there, I was kept there until the next day.'' She swiveled her chair so she could look out the window at the Gulf. Nick was probably deep beneath the sea. She sent up a silent prayer that he was safe. On the other hand, she didn't exactly wish him well, either. Damn him. At the very least, he could have left her a note. "It was one of those things that you kind of had to be there to understand.''

"Uh-huh. Well, *this* is what I understand. You got yourself into a situation that made Des feel he needed to step in and help you.''

She slowly smiled. "You sound upset. What's the matter? Jealous that you didn't come up with the idea first?''

"Frankly, yes.''

Tess chuckled. "Well, you don't have to worry. I turned down Des's offer of help.''

"So I heard. And I've got just one question. *Why?*''

"Because I was in no danger. And because I knew that, one way or another, I could get home by that afternoon.''

"Still, Tess. You passed up a golden opportunity to get Des all to yourself, and I don't understand why, unless it was somehow part of your scheme.''

"I can't explain it to you, Jill, but know this. I have no scheme to get Des, not yesterday, not today.''

For a couple of moments there was silence. Then, "It was that guy at your birthday party, wasn't it? The one you danced with?''

"That's the one.''

"He was interesting, all right, but, Tess...*Des.*''

She had no intention of telling Jill the truth, that she'd

fallen so madly in love with Nick that now she could never marry another man, not even if that man did come with fifty percent of Baron International attached to him. But to lighten her mood, if only temporarily, she decided to give Jill a hard time. "Hey, did you ever think I might be using the old hard-to-get ruse on Des?"

"Are you?"

"Sorry. My methods are top secret. But I will say that Des was *very* worried about me. In fact, he told me some things that he's never said to me before. Things about the way he feels about me. Really *lovely* things." It was all true, though not in the ways she was implying. It was also guaranteed to put Jill into a tailspin.

"Bitch."

She nearly laughed out loud. "Why, Jill—such *language.*"

"Never mind my language. You've got worse problems. Since it doesn't look as if you're going to be able to meet the will's conditions by your deadline, you're obviously pinning all your hopes on Des. But let me tell you something. I wouldn't do that, if I were you. The game is far from over."

"What can I say, Jill?" she asked, infusing her tone with brightness. "You're absolutely right. Now, you have a really great day. Goodbye."

She hung up the phone and dropped her face into her hands. The elation over getting the best of Jill had vanished even more quickly than she'd expected it to, and regret had rushed in to replace it. She shouldn't have baited her sister like she had, but it was a habit of a lifetime, a habit encouraged by their father.

What would it be like to be as close to her sisters as Nick was to Kathie? After all, Jill and Kit were the only two people in the world who really understood the pressures under which they'd been raised—the pressure to measure up to their father's standards, the pressure to constantly compete and best one another. Sharing their emotions and feelings with one another might lighten some of the load the three of them carried on their individual shoulders.

But would that even be possible? She tried to envision a situation that would allow harmony to exist among them, and couldn't. Perhaps a few years down the road, if she and Kit were able to meet their father's goal for them and were able to join Jill in an equal partnership in the company, they could forget about their stupid competition. But for that to happen, Des would have to marry someone other than Jill or Kit or Tess. And the three of them would have to let go of a lot of old habits, along with years of hurtful words and deeds.

Even then, she couldn't envision them ever being as close as Kathie and Nick were. But would it be possible, she wondered, for them to find their way to at least some sort of amicable relationship?

It would be tough, no question about it. However, she'd once heard the longest journey began with one step. She swiveled her chair to her desk and placed her hand on the phone. If she called Jill back and apologized for baiting her, it might be a good first step.

The phone rang beneath her hand and she jumped.

"It's Vega," Ron called from the next room.

She let out a long, steadying breath, then picked up the phone. "Good morning, Jimmy. Give me some good news."

"As a matter of fact, I can do just that. The storm didn't touch us."

"Great."

"We got some of the fireworks and a little of the wind, but in the end, it was nothing to speak of."

"That *is* good news. That also means the ocean floor wouldn't have been disturbed, right?"

"If it was, it was minimal. Why?"

"An acquaintance of mine has a diving site nearby."

"Oh, yeah, I've seen the support ship as I've flown back and forth. What's he diving for?"

"There's a shipwreck down there that he's interested in, and it's in a precarious position on a scarp. If anything happens on our rig that might affect the ship, let me know, will you?"

"Sure. I keep you informed anyway."

"I know, and thanks."

Tess spent the rest of the day in her typical high-speed mode, doing what she did every day, making decisions, reading reports, solving problems. Her business interests ranged the world. She had to constantly monitor not only the condition and output of the wells themselves, but she had to make sure her working relationships with the countries and the politicians she did business with remained good.

But no matter how busy she stayed, or how hard she tried, she couldn't forget Nick or the night they'd spent together. From the start, their combined chemistry had been volatile. Last night it had finally exploded. And the explosion had been beyond her wildest imagination.

There had been times she couldn't breathe because the ecstasy was so strong. Then, just when she didn't think she could go any farther or reach any higher, he had proved her wrong and showed her there was yet another level of rapture to reach.

She'd infused every moment they'd spent together, every movement, every touch, every kiss, with her love. But just because she'd fallen in love with Nick didn't mean she'd completely lost her ability to think. When it came to sex, he was a master, a magician, but he didn't love her.

He seemed to have finally accepted that she wasn't going to change her mind about the drilling, but even if he hadn't, it didn't matter. It wouldn't change one thing that had happened last night.

To him, it had been sex. To her, it had been love. But both of them had experienced the same deep, immeasurable, intense fulfillment and satisfaction. Those kinds of emotions couldn't be faked.

And then, while she'd slept, he had left, without a word or a note, or any sign that he would ever return.

As the day drew to a close, she let Ron leave work early for a date with his new girlfriend, but she continued to work until her eyes blurred and her shoulders ached and she had no choice but to stop.

Once in her bedroom, she slowly undressed, then sank into a tub of hot, scented water, leaned her head back and closed her eyes. She was tired, but she was used to being tired. She hurt, and to a certain extent she was used to hurting. But she'd never known what pain was until she'd awakened this morning, alone. And she didn't know how to make the pain go away.

The perfumed scent of bathwater drew Nick through the bedroom and into the bathroom. At the sight of Tess, his breath caught in his throat and he came to a standstill. She lay in the tub, her eyes closed, her arms floating on the fragrant oiled water, her legs stretched out. She looked relaxed, but not completely.

He'd seen her face at the moment of climax, when she'd let go of everything except him. But now, though any other person might not be able to detect it, he could see the tiny lines of tension on her face. They bothered him. Yet the memory of last night, the sight of her now, had him hardening.

Her skin glowed sleekly with a faint rose color. Her blond hair was pinned atop her head, but at the back of her neck, tendrils had escaped, and the moisture had tightened them into small, beguiling curls. Her breasts rose halfway out of the water, her nipples so soft he could almost taste their sweetness.

He had to fight the urge to kneel beside the tub, lean over and pull her nipples into his mouth one at a time. With one suck he knew he could have them tight and her breasts throbbing for more. He wasn't bragging. It was fact. After last night, he knew her body inside and out.

He hadn't meant to return to her tonight.

That first night he'd met her, he'd tried his best to resist her, but somewhere inside him, he'd known that before he would be satisfied, he was going to have to have her. Still, he'd tried to fight his growing need for her.

She'd admitted that she thought his pursuit of her was to coerce her into doing what he wanted. But she gave him way too much credit.

Truthfully, there wasn't much he wouldn't do to make his grandpa's dream come true. He'd crisscrossed the country many times to get the needed backing. He'd worked for years, pushing himself mentally and physically, to get to where he was now, shoring up the ship so the true excavation could begin. But he would never, ever willingly hurt Tess.

Yet that was just what he was doing.

She'd made it too easy for him. She was entirely too desirable. She'd unconsciously molded herself against him when they'd danced. She'd responded to his kisses with the fire of someone who had never been truly kissed before.

And when they'd made love, she'd gone up in flames and taken him with her.

Still, in no way was it her fault. His original plan had been simply to get one-on-one time with her so he could tell her his story. But when he'd seen her, complicated needs and desires had clouded his intent.

He'd wanted to hold her, so he'd asked her to dance. He'd wanted to taste her and feel her soft lips, so he'd kissed her. He'd wanted to have her, so last night he'd finally taken her to bed. And still it wasn't enough for him. He wanted more.

He couldn't explain what he was feeling to himself. How could he explain it to her? Besides, under the circumstances, anything he told her would be suspect.

Tess opened her eyes and looked up at him. Immediately her expression turned wary. "I didn't think you'd be coming back."

"To be honest, I wasn't sure myself. But it turned out...I had to."

She hesitated, expression after expression chasing across her face too quickly for him to read them. Then, slowly, she lifted her arms to him. "Join me."

He began tearing at his clothes, unable to get them off fast enough. He knew that soon the day would come when he would pay for his greediness, but right now all he could think of was his all-consuming need for her. He slipped into the scented water, then into her.

The next morning, Ron answered the phone, then called out, "It's Kit."

She smiled. Chances were, the news about Des offering to rescue her had finally reached her younger sister. Remembering her thoughts of yesterday about trying to be close with her sisters, she decided to try something new—

being nice. Kit wasn't as hard-boiled as Jill. Instead she was wild as the land she governed and rebellious as a west Texas storm. Tess never knew which way she would jump.

She reached for the phone. "Good morning, Kit. How are you today?"

"Cut out the Mary Sunshine crap. I'm not interested."

Tess looked at the ceiling, searching for divine guidance. She found none.

"I heard about the ruse you tried to pull on Des."

"It wasn't a ruse, Kit. Besides, you don't have to worry. I didn't take him up on his offer."

"But you made him *think* about you, which, as we know, is half the battle with him."

"I—" Automatically she started to defend herself, but Kit sounded as unhappy as she'd ever heard her. "Kit, what's the matter?"

"Oh, gee, Tess, I don't know. What could be wrong? I've got the best job in the world, running this ranch, and I simply couldn't be happier."

"Then why do you sound so *un*happy? Are you worried about making the will's goal? You've got two more years, you know."

"That stupid will is the last thing I'd worry about."

"Okay." Obviously Kit had gotten up on the wrong side of the bed this morning. "Anything else I can do for you today?"

"Yeah. Lay off Des."

"Okay."

There was stunned silence on the other end. Then, "Did you just agree to stop running after Des?"

"I've never run after Des, Kit, but yes, basically that's what I agreed to."

"Why?"

There was no point in bringing Nick into the explanation.

Nick had walked into her life as suddenly as he would one day walk out of it. And, as usual, she would be left to deal with her pain alone. "I've decided that if I can meet the will's demands, I'll be perfectly satisfied to have my one-sixth of the company."

"You're kidding, right?"

"No, Kit, I'm honestly not. As it is, I'm going to have enough of a battle to meet Father's conditions. But even though I may be going right down to the wire with it, I believe I can. After that, I don't want to wage any more battles. I'll be happy."

"If you're serious, that's the most amazing thing I've ever heard."

"I couldn't be more serious. Anything else?"

"No. I guess that's it. But, Tess?"

"Yes?"

"Good luck."

She smiled. Admittedly, Kit's tone when she'd wished her luck had been somewhat reluctant, but it didn't change the fact that she had said the word. She would take it. "Thank you. Talk to you later."

"Yeah, sure. Bye."

Tess hung up the phone, still smiling.

The phone rang again. This time it was Jimmy Vega. "Hi, Jimmy."

"Hi. Just called to report that things are finally settling down and going our way. No broken drill bits or equipment. The last few days have been smooth as silk."

"Great. That's music to my ears. Now if we can just hit the oil on schedule..."

"It'll be a couple more months, but I've got my money on your instincts. There's a lot of oil down there, and we're heading right for it."

"Thanks for the confidence, Jimmy. Talk to you later."

After hanging up, Tess leaned back in her chair. She ticked off the good things that had happened so far this morning. Kit had done the previously unheard of thing of actually wishing her good luck. Jimmy had called to report good news. And then there had been last night.

Nick had showed up and made love to her with an intensity that had been even stronger than the night before. But once again, when she awoke this morning, he was gone.

That night became a routine that was repeated over and over.

Just when she was certain Nick wouldn't show up, he did, hungry for her. Without words, they would fall on the bed and make love until they were both exhausted.

Even after their lovemaking, they never said much to each other. She didn't ask how his work was going, and he didn't question her about her drilling. But their tacit agreement to focus on lovemaking and forget about any other subject encompassed far more than their respective jobs. Anything personal was also strictly off-limits.

Tess knew why *she* remained silent. She was afraid that her words would in some way reveal to him how very much she loved him. She was convinced that if he were to find out, he would disappear even faster than he eventually would anyway. As to why he remained silent, it was no doubt as simple as her reason was. He didn't want to say anything that she might misconstrue as a commitment.

And so it continued, days of work, nights of passion. During the day, when rational thought was possible, she tried to warn herself to remain more objective about what was happening between Nick and her. But during the nights, when he held her in his arms, she would realize that she was already so deeply in love with him, and so desperate with wanting him, that when he left, she probably wouldn't survive.

The night was bright, with a full moon. Its light illuminated the terrace with a silver brilliance and streamed through the French doors into Tess's bedroom, providing light for the two entwined lovers as they lay on the bed, facing each other, recovering from an exhausting bout of lovemaking. Only the waves of the Gulf breaking onto the shore, along with their ragged breathing, interrupted the silence of the night.

Nick held Tess to him with a possessiveness that surprised even him. But then, right from the first, nothing about his feelings for Tess had been normal. He was still inside her and he didn't want to pull out. As long as he remained inside her, he could pretend she was his. And as long as she remained content to be held, he planned not to break the connection.

Slowly, gently, so as not to startle her, he lifted a hand and pushed her damp hair away from her face. "Are you sleepy?"

"I'm tired," she replied softly, "but not ready to go to sleep yet."

"You work long hours." He was very aware that he'd just crossed a line that had been drawn by both of them, though it hadn't been intentional. Thinking only of her, he had been trying to find out if he should leave her alone and let her go to sleep.

"Yes." Her answer was short and simple.

His hand lightly followed the smooth curves of her waist and hips. "I've been wondering about something."

She moved, breaking the sexual connection that he'd wanted to maintain as long as possible. "What's that?" she asked, rolling over on her back and stretching like a cat.

Desire stirred in his loins, but he did his best to ignore it, something that with Tess was almost impossible. Still, he tried. "The first night we met—it was your birthday party."

She looked at him, a faint smile on her lips. "I remember."

"From a couple of remarks I overheard, I gather it's an annual event, with only the party's location changing from year to year."

"Right. The change of location keeps it fresh and fun."

"I also gathered that you're the one who throws the party."

"Uh-huh." She raised an arm and rested it on the pillow above her head. The movement lifted her breast.

He had to consciously make himself stare into her eyes. "Why?"

"Why what?"

"Why do you have to throw your own birthday party? What about your family? Or your friends?"

Her brow puckered, and she didn't answer him right away. The silence stretched out so long, he wasn't sure she was going to answer him.

Finally, though, she spoke. "I suppose either Kathie or your grandmother throws you a party every year?"

He grinned. "Yeah, they do. Even though I'd just as soon not make a big deal out of it, it's important to them."

"Did you have a party every year when you were growing up?"

The question surprised him. "Of course. Doesn't every kid?"

"Yes," she said in a tone that made him think she was answering the question with extra care. "Were your parties fun?"

"Yeah. Sure."

"With cake and ice cream and gifts?"

"That's what a birthday party is, isn't it?"

She swallowed. "Back to your original question, I enjoy throwing my own parties. It's the only way I can insure that everything is just as I like it."

"So what you're basically admitting is that you're a control freak." He'd meant the comment to be funny, but she didn't smile.

"I suppose so. Anyway, why all the questions about my birthday parties?"

"I just thought it was odd that you throw your own parties, that's all."

"Not everyone was raised the way you and Kathie were raised, Nick."

"What do you mean?"

She shook her head. "Never mind."

"Are you saying you weren't given birthday parties when you were growing up?"

"The lady who has worked for my uncle for years always baked me a cake. She did the same for my sisters. And that's the last thing I'd like to say on that particular subject. I think I'm sleepy now."

"Hey," he said softly. "I didn't mean to dredge up any sad memories."

"Don't worry. You didn't."

But he had, he thought. He would give money to know the true story, but he would probably never hear it. One of these nights, when he walked into her bedroom, she was going to tell him to leave. It might be after they struck oil on the rig and she was getting ready to return to her Dallas office. Or it might even be sooner. Quite simply, she could grow tired of him arriving every night and expecting her to welcome him with open arms.

With their objectives so diametrically opposed, it was a

wonder she even let him through the door. But she reveled in their lovemaking as much as he did. Pure and simple, they pleasured each other, though pleasure was too tame a word for the passion they ignited in each other night after night.

But he wasn't kidding himself. Soon she would either leave Corpus or grow tired of him. Or both. She had a whole other life in Dallas. As for him, if he got lucky, and nothing happened on her rig to disturb the *Águila*'s site, he would be in Corpus for the next few years. After that, he would return to Austin and his teaching.

He couldn't see a future for the two of them, but his need for her continued to grow. Consequently, each night when he drove into her, he could feel himself becoming more and more desperate.

If only there was some way to make her need him as much as he needed her. If only there was some way to make her his permanently. But there was nothing he had that she wanted. Besides, she was too independent. If nothing else, the fact that she threw her own birthday parties told him that.

Their worlds were completely different, except when they were in bed. Here they could shut out the world. The problem was, he knew he couldn't count on this relative peace to continue for much longer.

# Ten

Tess stood at her office window, staring at the Gulf, wondering what Nick was doing at that exact moment. It was a familiar position for her. Every minute of every day, she worried about him. Each night, when he came to her, it took all her willpower to resist begging him to give up the deep-water diving.

But how could she expect him to give up trying to attain his goal when she wasn't willing to give up trying to reach hers?

She hadn't done any research on the subject, yet common sense told her that the use of submersibles was the safest way to go. True, something from the ship could fall on the submersible and trap both it and the person inside it. But the danger of that happening was minuscule compared to the inherent dangers of the diving Nick was doing.

She'd flown out to the rig yesterday, and the helicopter had passed over Nick's support ship. The divers' flag had been up. When he'd come to her last night, it had taken every last ounce of willpower she possessed to keep from begging him to stop diving. She hadn't done it, but she hadn't been able to stop herself from clinging to him a little harder.

She heard the phone ring on Ron's desk and returned to her chair just as Ron called to her. "It's Vega."

She picked up the phone. "Hi, Jimmy. Everything going okay?"

"It is now, but, Tess, a little while ago we came as close to a blowout as I've ever been or want to be again."

She could feel the blood drain from her face. "Oh, my God. What happened?"

"We drilled into an unexpected high pressure pocket, and if I hadn't been there watching the instruments, it could have been disaster."

"Thank God you caught it in time."

"Yeah."

She shut her eyes. "Jimmy..."

"I know. Believe me, I know."

She couldn't think of any words adequate enough, but then, with Jimmy she didn't have to. He knew the ramifications as well as she did, probably even better.

If a blowout had occurred, it would have been a disaster too horrible to contemplate. Any pipes or equipment in the bore hole would have come shooting out with enough pressure to cause a catastrophe of massive proportions. In addition, any fuel or gas in the bore hole would have been propelled to the surface and ignited into an instant fire that would have created an explosion big enough to kill everyone on the rig.

And if Nick had been diving, he would also have been killed. His death would have been caused by the percussion of the explosion or by the ocean floor earthquake or by flying pipes and equipment that, if they had enough force behind them, could have reached him. Any one of the three things would have been enough to kill him, and it very well could have been all three.

The earthquake alone would have sent both him and the *Águila* plunging over the side of the scarp into the abyss. And when the *Águila* finally came to rest, Nick's body would have been buried, his lifeline cut.

Jimmy kept talking, but her mind was on Nick.

When she hung up, she was shaking. She quickly filled Ron in, then asked him to hold all her calls. She went to the terrace and stared at the point on the horizon where she knew Nick's crew and ship were. God, if it hadn't been for Jimmy's fast action, Nick would almost certainly have been killed today.

She started to pace, her mind locked on the horror of what had almost happened. With today's modern technology, blowouts were very rare. Unfortunately, though, the very genuine possibility still existed.

They'd already known they were drilling in an overpressurized zone, and they'd been prepared. But they'd also known that the conditions the drill encountered could change within a few meters and they could hit a pocket that contained an even higher amount of pressure than was the norm for their site, which was exactly what had happened today. It was why everyone on the rig had to stay on their toes at all times. It was also why she'd hired Jimmy Vega as her supervisor. He was the best.

She lost track of how many times she paced the length of the terrace and back. She had no idea what time it was. Fear had her in a viselike grip. Her mind was spinning, racing, but always it returned to the same subject. If Nick had been killed today...

Suddenly she whirled and returned to her office. Without

a word to Ron, she placed a call to Jimmy. When he answered, she didn't hesitate. "I want the drilling stopped now, Jimmy. *Now.*"

"What?"

"I want it stopped for at least two months."

"Tess, are you crazy? We had a close call today, but—"

"Listen to me, Jimmy. Stop the drilling now. Keep all personnel on the payroll. Make up a schedule so that you have a maintenance crew working on the rig at all times, but rotate them so that everyone will have a chance for a paid vacation."

"Tess, what in the hell is going on? I thought—"

"And you thought right, but this is just something I have to do for now, and I won't explain it. Two months, Jimmy. Then, at the end of that time, we'll start back up again at full speed. So make sure the rig is ready to go at that time."

"Sure. Okay, but…?"

He sounded bewildered, and she couldn't blame him. "You did a great job today, Jimmy. Arrange it so that you can get in some vacation time, too. In the meantime, I'll be in contact, and I'll definitely be back in two months." She hung up the phone and stared at it. She'd just cut her own throat.

"Tess?"

She glanced up. Ron was standing in the doorway of her office, looking thunderstruck. "You heard?"

He nodded. "Do you know what you're doing?"

She flashed him a rueful smile. "Unfortunately, I do. Pack up. I want to be ready to leave here in an hour."

"Where are we going?"

"Dallas, to start with."

Nick climbed the steps to the terrace. It had been a brutal day, and all he could think of was getting to Tess. He could think of nothing he would like better than to soak in a nice hot bath with her, then make slow, hot love until steam was coming off the water. He smiled in anticipation.

The lights were off in Tess's bedroom, he noticed, but that wasn't unusual. Maybe she was already in the tub, waiting for him, with candles lit. But her French doors were closed. That *was* unusual.

He turned the handle, and the door opened. "Tess?" He looked around for a light switch and found it. The room was quiet, and Tess was no where to be seen. "Tess?"

He walked into the bathroom. The tub was empty. The area on the marble counter where she kept her makeup and perfume was bare. A chill crawled down his spine. An investigation of her closet revealed that almost three-fourths of her clothes were missing. Had a sudden business trip come up? He'd given her the phone number on his support ship. Why hadn't she called him to tell him where she was going?

Then he saw it. An envelope was propped up on one of the pillows on the bed. He tore it open and read. *I've ordered the drilling stopped for two months. I hope that will give you the time you need.*

Stupefied, he stared at the paper. She hadn't even bothered signing it.

*"Guadalupe!"* he bellowed, striding angrily out of the bedroom and through the house. "Guadalupe!"

"Yes, sir?" An apprehensive Guadalupe appeared.

"Where did Miss Baron go?"

"I don't know."

"She didn't tell any of the staff?"

"No, sir."

"Then did she say when she would return?"

She nodded. "In two months."

Nick let out a string of oaths that had Guadalupe backing

up. As soon as he saw her reaction, he stopped. "I'm sorry, Guadalupe. I apologize." He let out a long, shaky breath. "Do you have any other information about her? Did she say anything, perhaps even something small, that might help me know where she went?"

"No." Despite his apology, Guadalupe continued to eye him cautiously.

"Okay. Thank you."

Guadalupe turned to leave.

"Wait. Please, could you get me a pen and piece of paper? I want to give you a number so that if you hear anything from Ms. Baron, anything at all, you can call and tell me. Okay?"

She nodded and went off to get the pen and paper.

Now that the rig had stopped drilling, Nick could do what he had to do with the assurance that, if anything went wrong, it wouldn't come from outside forces. It was up to him to continue to make sure his operation ran safely. But keeping his mind on his work was much harder than he would have expected.

The days were difficult, but the nights were impossible. He ached, he missed Tess so much, and he spent a lot of time taking cold showers that did absolutely no good.

At first he tried to track her down. He called her Dallas office and spoke to the now all-too familiar Ron, but according to Ron, she wasn't there. When Nick pushed, the assistant finally told him that Tess was making an inspection tour of all her business sites. When he asked for her itinerary, Ron informed him that Tess had specifically asked that it not be given to him.

He attempted to reach her two sisters. At first he was rebuffed, but after telling each of their assistants that he was calling about Tess, he was put through. Jill took the news of Tess's abrupt departure strangely. She muttered something about Tess crying wolf one too many times, and that this time, she was going to call Des herself and tell him not to bother. Then she'd hung up. Kit's response had been one he could better understand. She'd simply informed him that if Ron had said Tess had gone off on a business trip, then that was where she'd gone, but that no, she didn't have a clue where she would be.

Those short conversations had left Nick frustrated. He couldn't believe that Tess's trip had been a planned one. If it had been, then why hadn't she told him? What had happened to cause her to bolt?

Had he done something wrong? Said something that hurt her? He searched his mind for some sort of clue but could find nothing. His memory of their last night together was strong. As usual, their time in each other's arms had consisted of sheer, unadulterated pleasure, and they'd both been left sated and drowsy.

Afterward, she had fallen asleep in his arms. He remembered he'd watched her for a while, listening to her breathe, something he'd done before. It was such a simple pleasure and one he'd never bothered to analyze.

After their lovemaking, when all the energy had been drained from her, she slept with the peace of a child. It was the only time he ever saw her truly relaxed. He didn't need to think twice to know she was under pressure she never talked about.

He'd always understood that by asking her to stop the drilling, he was asking her to give up an enormous amount of money that would have a long, long line of zeros in it. And he'd known that if she agreed, it would be a sacrifice that would show up on her profit-and-loss statement at the end of the year. But he'd also known it wouldn't come near to breaking her financially.

Plus, although he could be wrong, he'd never received the impression that it was financial greed that kept her drilling. He'd taunted her with that at the beginning, but after he'd gotten to know her, he'd come to the conclusion that there was something else at the core of it all. But no matter how he'd poked and prodded at her, trying to figure out why she wouldn't give an inch on the matter, he hadn't been able to get any closer to an answer he could understand.

The night after he'd contacted Tess's two sisters, he went to her house. Guadalupe let him in.

"Thank you." He made a point of smiling at her. "I'm not going to stay long."

She nodded, her demeanor formal. "Is there anything I can get you while you are here?"

"No." Then he hastened to add, "Thank you, anyway."

With another nod, she disappeared.

He slowly walked through the big main living room with its walls of windows that overlooked the terrace, the sloping green lawn and the Gulf beyond. But it wasn't the view he was there for. In fact, he wasn't entirely sure why he was there. He just wanted to be where Tess had been and where the two of them had been together.

But there was an empty feel about the whole house. By rights, it shouldn't feel so deserted, because he knew the staff was there, and all the rooms looked just as they had when Tess had been there, giving the impression that she would walk in at any minute. But the house still felt empty.

In her bedroom, he sat on the end of the bed and looked around. God, he would give anything, do anything, to have her back with him here. Physically, he craved her in the worst possible way, his body felt tormented with need for her. But surprisingly, his desire for her went beyond the physical. Emotionally, he realized, he needed simply to cradle her in his arms and hold her with no sex in mind.

*He loved her.*

There it was, out in the open at last. He'd finally let himself admit what his heart and soul must have secretly known for a long while. He was in love with Tess.

In all probability his heart had been lost the moment he first laid eyes on her. Then he'd possessed her and found that he couldn't get enough of her. Even when he'd been mad as hell at her, he'd still wanted her. But he'd never let himself think beyond that point.

Things had settled into something of a routine with them. Each night he'd showed up here and she'd opened her arms to welcome him. He'd known that it wouldn't last. He'd also known he wanted to find a way to keep her with him, but he hadn't thought of being in love with her. For some reason, it just never occurred to him. He lived in the present with her. He lived for the nights they spent together.

Then she'd disappeared from his life, and in the process of trying to figure out what had happened, he hadn't had any choice but to face the truth, and when he did, he wondered why it had taken him so long to figure it out. He loved her. He wanted to spend the rest of his life with her, each day, each night. He *had* to have her back.

If only he could find something that would help him make sense of why she'd left in the first place. And, maybe more importantly, he needed to understand why she had finally decided to stop drilling.

The last time they'd talked about it had been the night of the storm. She'd told him then in no uncertain terms that she couldn't stop. Yet now she had.

Why? He shoved himself off the bed and began to pace. Could it conceivably be that she'd made the decision because she'd fallen in love with him? That thought stopped him in his tracks. But if that had been the reason, why in the hell had she left?

No, she couldn't possibly be in love him. She'd never shared any of herself with him other than the physical. She was too independent. She'd left too abruptly. She didn't, couldn't love him.

But facts were definitely missing.

As much as he'd told her and showed her about himself and his reasons for wanting to preserve the *Águila* and harvest the gold, she'd never once hinted at the reason she couldn't stop the drilling. There had to be something more at stake than money. Except now she'd given the decision to stop. Had that something, whatever it was, simply gone away or ceased to be vital?

He shook his head. No matter which route he took with his thoughts, there wasn't one damn thing about any of this that made sense.

He moved around the bed and grabbed the phone. After punching in his credit card number, he dialed the number of an old college friend who worked as a journalist for the *Dallas Morning News*. Without preamble, he asked him for a favor.

The next morning he was at work at the *Águila*. For whatever reason, Tess had given him this gift of two months. He didn't plan to waste a minute of it. Besides, the one thing he was positive of was that in less than two months she would return.

It was good to be back, Tess reflected, as she unpacked her suitcases. If nothing else, returning to the house in Corpus Christi and settling in meant that she could finally stay in one place for longer than three days. And she was way past ready for that. She'd had enough of hotels and airplanes.

She'd already been in contact with Jimmy Vega and given the order to resume drilling first thing in the morning. Though she didn't know whether she'd given Nick enough time to finish shoring up the ship, she'd given him most of the time he'd asked for, and that was all she could do.

Now she would have to sweat out the next few months and pray like hell that they would strike oil. After that, she wasn't sure what would be possible in regards to meeting the will's condition. She just knew one thing. Giving up was not in her genes.

"Hello, Tess."

She whirled. "Nick." She was stunned. "How did you know I was back?"

"I didn't know for sure." He walked slowly through the open French doors, his gaze fixed firmly on her. "But during the last few days there's been increased activity out at your rig. I've checked here each night since."

"How did you know about the increased activity? You can't see the rig from your site."

"Helicopter flights increased, plus I would drive the runabout out a bit so I could use binoculars."

"Oh." She turned to her unpacking, trying not to think too hard about how her heart had jumped when she'd seen him or how fast it was pounding. She forced herself to take a deep, calming breath.

During the last two months she'd spent long, lonely, sleepless nights, trying to push all thoughts of Nick from her mind. It had been useless. Her body had constantly ached for him, and her mind had retained perfect recall of every moment she'd spent with him. But most of all, her heart had hurt because of her love for him that would never be returned.

Now he was here, standing in front of her, dressed at his most casual in jeans and a dark teal T-shirt. With the dark color so close to his face, the already vivid color of his amber eyes was more pronounced, their strength more piercing.

"Your grandparents—are they both okay?"

"Yes."

"How's the *Águila*? Have you been able to shore it up sufficiently?"

"It's as good as it's going to get. Why did you leave, Tess?"

She could feel the waves of his anger surging toward her. It was almost like the night of the storm, when they'd first made love. Then it had been waves of lust and passion that had overwhelmed her. Now it was anger, and she had very few weapons against it. The only thing she could do to protect herself was try to keep her guard up.

She hadn't gone through two months of hell only to once again be caught up in a maelstrom of passion. She still loved him, maybe even more than when she'd left. But over the past two months, she'd attempted to scrape together every last ounce of objectivity she could manage about him. The result was that she'd come to an important conclusion. If she let her guard down and once again accepted him as her lover, there would be nothing left of her heart or of her but pieces when he walked out her door for the final time.

He didn't love her, and one day soon he would grow tired of her. If not tonight, then perhaps six weeks from now. If not six weeks, then perhaps six months. But when it came right down to it, it really didn't matter when it happened. She had to remain strong, stop any passion before it started and convince him that she wasn't interested in resuming where they'd left off.

She pulled a couple of dresses from her suitcase and hung them in the closet. "Once I gave the order to stop the drilling, there was no reason for me to stay here. I made

the decision that my time would be better spent elsewhere.''

''And you didn't think I'd be even mildly interested in
that decision?''

She'd known that sooner or later this confrontation
would come. She'd hoped she could have a chance to settle
in and catch her breath first. She glanced at him, then away.
She reached into the suitcase and pulled out a pant suit. ''I
thought you'd be happy. I made the decision you wanted.
I also left you the note, telling you so. After that...'' She
gave a nonchalant shrug.

He placed his hands on his hips, and his amber eyes
flashed dark fire. ''Okay, Tess, let's cut right through the
crap. I'll concede the fact that your business is far-flung
and that you felt, since you'd stopped the drilling here, that
your time could be better spent elsewhere. That makes perfect business sense.''

She tensed for the next volley she knew would come and
it came fast.

''But damn it, Tess—what about *us?*''

She bent to reach for a sweater, paused for a fraction of
a second, then lifted it out of the case and straightened,
certain he hadn't noticed her pause. ''I don't like good-
byes.''

He exhaled a long breath, then walked to the dresser
where, before he'd arrived, she'd absently tossed a camisole, meaning to put it in the drawer later. He picked it up
and rubbed the silk and lace material between his thumb
and fingers.

''Okay,'' he said, continuing to finger the camisole,
''let's go another way. I lost count of the times you told
me no. So what happened to make you change your
mind?''

The sight of him fingering the camisole, an intimate undergarment that had been against her skin, unnerved her. She walked over and carefully took it from him. "I'm not sure what you want me to say, Nick. You worked long and hard to get me to make the decision you wanted. So I made it. But now it's not enough for you? Remember that, thanks to you, I met your grandparents. They touched me. I liked them a great deal. And I just kept thinking about them." She shrugged again, as if, in the end, her decision had been easy. "Finally I decided it was the right thing to do."

Nodding, he leaned against the dresser and crossed his arms over his chest. Watching him, she saw something that made her pause. There was an ever-so-slight change in him that she might have missed if she hadn't been keeping such a careful eye on him. Still, she couldn't identify what was different about him. It could very well be her imagination.

"I have something I need to tell you, Tess. I called up an old friend about a week after you left. He was one of my roommates in college, but now he's an investigative reporter for the *Dallas Morning News*."

Tension and dread gripped her as she anticipated what he would say next.

"He has more resources at his command than I do, so I asked him as a favor to dig around and see what he could find out about your family, its background, the company and…you."

Anger rushed through her, extinguishing the dread. Depending on what he'd learned, the knowledge could leave her completely vulnerable to him—something she couldn't afford. "Just what in the hell gave you the right to do such a thing? I had *done* what you asked. Why couldn't you simply let it be?"

"Because it didn't make sense to me and I needed it to. I—" He gestured vaguely. "Obviously the reason you made the decision was for me and my family. Except right from the first, you'd been so adamant that you *couldn't*. I needed to find out what had changed.''

She pointed at him, her anger so great she was almost shaking. "If I'd known you were going to invade my privacy, not to mention my family's, I would *never* have stopped the drilling, and you and the *Águila* be damned.''

"Believe me," he said, his expression grave, "I knew when I made the request of Jerry that you wouldn't like it.'' He paused, as if giving careful consideration to what he would say next. "But at the time, I just thought I'd get an explanation that would satisfy me, and that would be that.''

She pointed again, this time to the open French doors. "Get out.''

He shook his head. "I'll go, but not yet. First I want to tell you what I found out, because there's still something I don't understand.''

"And you think I care?" Her hands clenched and unclenched at her side. "God, Nick. You got the drilling stopped. You even had me for a while. Why wasn't that enough for you?''

With Nick, her emotions had always run high, but she'd never expected anger. Now, though, she was practically choking with it. The thing she feared the most was to have her feelings for him laid bare. That would leave her absolutely defenseless. And she had this awful feeling that that was exactly what was about to happen.

He moved his hand in a pacifying gesture, and once again she thought she caught a glimpse of something different about him. Her curiosity was just enough to stop her from going over and bodily pushing him out the door.

"I found out that when you ordered the drilling stopped, you made a far greater sacrifice than I ever could have imagined. In fact, I'm staggered by it.''

He'd found out about the clause in the will. After that, it wouldn't have taken a rocket scientist to figure out why she'd given the order. She waited for what he would say next, dreading the sound of pity that would fill his voice.

But instead of saying anything, he slipped his hands into the pockets of his jeans, then brought them out again, glanced toward the terrace for several moments, then at her, a frown on his face.

That was when she realized what was different about him. He was *uncertain* about something. She'd never seen him hesitate about anything. He'd always been completely assured, even when he'd maneuvered her into the position of having to spend the night at his grandparents' house.

He glanced at his feet, then looked at her. "Why, Tess? Why would you make such a huge sacrifice for me?" He gestured, and this time she thought she saw his hand tremble. He stared at her, his brow furrowed. "As I understand it, because of your decision, it's now almost one hundred percent certain that you'll lose your part of your family's company. You *needed* that time you gave me. God, Tess, why didn't you tell me? If I'd known..."

Her knees suddenly weak, she sank onto her bed. If he had figured out that she loved him, her decision would make sense to him. Yet he was still saying he didn't understand, which meant she still had a shot at keeping her feelings to herself. "Believe it or not, Nick, I have a heart." She made her tone very matter-of-fact. "The day I made the decision, we came close to having a blowout on the rig. I decided I didn't want anyone's death on my conscience. Not your men, or you, or my crew. So I stopped all operations so that a complete maintenance check could be conducted." It wasn't a complete lie, and he just might buy it.

His shoulders slumped, once again something she wouldn't have noticed if she hadn't been watching him so carefully. Then, slowly, he walked around the bed and went down on bent knee in front of her.

He gazed up at her. "When you just left without saying goodbye, I felt like I'd been hit with a battering ram. I went a little crazy. Ron, as usual, was no help. I even called your sisters, trying to find out where you were, but they gave me the impression they couldn't have cared less." He reached for her hand and looked at it. "It's probably a good thing I didn't know where you were, because if I'd known, I would have gone after you instead of staying here and taking care of business."

He laced his fingers through hers. By doing that, it would make it harder for her to pull her hand from his, though she couldn't be sure if that was why he'd done it. She couldn't read him, not at all.

"Finally I calmed down," he said, his gaze searching her face, "and I realized I had no other alternative but to wait two months until you returned. That was when I started thinking. During the day I'd been focusing on the *Águila*, and at night I'd been coming here and focusing on you."

She could feel herself holding her breath. She had no idea what he was leading up to, but she could hear an uncertainty in his voice that matched the way he was acting.

"But when you disappeared, I had no choice but to stop and think about it. That's when I realized how vitally important you had become to me. And I figured out something I should have known from the beginning. I figured out I love you, Tess."

She was stunned. It was the last thing she'd expected to hear him say. Her fears had been unfounded. *He* was the one who was setting aside his pride and laying bare his heart, and she knew exactly how hard it was for him, because she knew exactly how hard it would be for her.

He hadn't guessed she loved him, she realized. How could he? From his point of view, she'd walked away from him without a backward glance. She hadn't even given him the courtesy of a phone call. She'd told Ron not to give him her itinerary. Now she understood his uncertainty.

He was opening himself up, telling her that he loved her without any reassurance that his love would be returned. It obviously hadn't occurred to him that the only reason she could have made such a decision was because she loved him.

In effect, she'd given up her part of the company for him, but he'd given up his pride for her. To her way of thinking, it was an even trade.

"Tess?"

Tears of pure bliss appeared unbidden in her eyes. She smiled unsteadily and squeezed his hand. "I can't begin to tell you how happy you've just made me, Nick. In fact, I'm overjoyed." She blinked away the tears. "I love you more than I can ever tell you."

"You…" He slowly shook his head, and a trace of wonderment entered his expression. "You're not just saying that, are you? Because if you are—"

"I wouldn't say something like that if it weren't true." She pulled her hand from his and tenderly framed his face. "Nick, I stopped the drilling because I couldn't bear the idea that I was putting you in even more danger than you already were. And I left because I badly needed some breathing space from you. I needed to find some objectivity, because I was afraid that if I stayed, I would eventually be so crushed when you left that I would never recover."

His expression solemn, he closed his fingers over her wrists and pulled her hands down to hold them. "God, Tess. I love you. I will never leave you. *Ever*. Please believe that."

She nodded, her eyes tearing once again with happiness. "I do."

He laughed, and to her surprise his eyes glistened with tears that matched her own. "You love me. I can hardly believe it. But..." He shook his head, and the tears disappeared. "Tess, the sacrifice you made. I don't completely understand all the whys and wherefores, but the part I do understand is that you've probably lost your portion of Baron International."

"It could very well turn out that way, though if I wanted, I could keep the job. But I'm not going to give up yet. While I've been away, I've had some time to think about that, too, and I may have a plan. I don't know if it will work or not, but—"

"What is it? I'll help you. I'll do anything you want."

She laughed lightly. "Then make love to me, right here, right now."

"But your plan—I want to help."

"I'll tell you about it later. Right now I need you more than I can say."

With a groan, he stood, and with one sweep of his arm, he cleared the bed. The suitcase fell off the end and the remaining clothes in it scattered, but neither of them noticed. She reached for him and pulled him onto the bed with her.

She kicked off her shoes, thinking that at last she knew what true happiness was. She felt exhilarated, and, at the same time, she felt completely at peace.

He shifted so they lay side by side. "I hope you realize that now that I know you love me, I'm never going to let you get away from me." His voice was husky, and his touch was tender as he traced the lines of her face and jaw. "I want to marry you and have babies with you and live the rest of my life with you. I want to grow old with you."

"We'll be a family," she said with soft elation. One day she would tell him how important that was to her, but not now. She slipped her hands under his T-shirt to feel the familiar warmth and smoothness of his back, and joy bubbled up in her and filled her voice. "And we'll spend part of every summer at your grandparents' farmhouse so that our children can run free and discover their own treasure. And we'll start our own wall of pictures, and we'll continue the tradition of growing your great-grandmother's irises, lots and lots of them that we'll pass on to our children for their homes."

His amber eyes shone bright as the sun. "By the way, even though you haven't said it, you will marry me."

She laughed, because it had been a statement, not a question. His uncertainty was gone and his self-assurance had returned. "Yes, Nick," she whispered, as she drew his head down to kiss him, "I will marry you."

# Epilogue

---

*Seven months later*

In her uncle's office on the Double B Ranch, Tess stood and handed one of the Baron International lawyers a check. "There it is—every penny required by my father's will, and four days early, I might add."

Uncle William smiled broadly from behind his desk. "Congratulations, Tess. I knew you'd do it."

She laughed. "Then you knew more than I did." She glanced at Nick, who was sitting to the left of her in one of the big easy chairs positioned in front of her uncle's desk. The pride beaming from his amber eyes and the rock-solid certainty that he loved her gave her a sense of security she'd never known before.

The rest of the family was there, as well. Des's chair was to her right. Jill sat on the other side of him. Kit was restlessly roaming the area behind the desk.

To her gratification, Des stood and reached over to give her a light, brief hug. "Let me add my congratulations to Dad's."

"Thank you."

Jill glanced pointedly at Nick. "I'm glad for you, Tess. It's just too bad you were put into a position where you had to sign away your rights to millions of dollars."

"Quit glaring at Nick," Tess said mildly. "If it's anyone's fault, it's Father's for making up that stupid clause in the first place. Besides, in the end I got exactly what was most important to me—my portion of the company *and* Nick."

Kit stopped her pacing, cocked a hip and frowned at Nick, then at Tess. "Still, you did give up an awful lot. And you were just plain lucky that Becca's husband works for one of the biggest oil companies in the world and was ready and willing to make you a deal. You could easily have lost it all."

"It was more than luck," Des said in quiet rebuke. "She chose Mel's company because he's a friend of hers, but any of the other big oil companies would have jumped at the chance."

Kit glared at Des, so Tess tried to divert her. "Turned out Mel and his company believed in me and my abilities more than my own father ever did. They're making the leap of faith that the well will pump enough oil over the years to make the money they paid me worthwhile."

Des rested his hand on Tess's shoulder. "You made an excellent deal, too. They not only paid you up front what you needed to satisfy the will, but they're also going to pay you a percentage of future royalties after they make back the advance."

"I suppose it's as good a deal as she could expect to make," Jill said, glaring at Des and at his hand on Tess's shoulder. "But she had to sign over the rights of something that had come about because of her own instincts and hard work."

Tess smiled at her sister. "Uh, was that by any chance a compliment?"

Jill's brow creased. "You know it's true, Tess. You're just like Kit and me. We never let go of anything that we've developed. Father taught us that. We keep what's ours, develop it as we see fit, then sit back and collect the money for the rest of the project's life. But because of your lost time, you had to give up the well, and in the end, you won't make nearly the money you would have if you'd been able to keep it."

"She's right," Kit said. "Have you calculated the money you're going to be losing?"

"Yes. But I've also calculated what I'll be gaining. I now have what should have been mine in the first place. Plus, I have something else that's far more valuable to me."

She reached for Nick's hand, and he stood. "We'd like to invite all of you to our wedding in two weeks. It's going to be a small ceremony, just for family, held in the little Uvalde church where Nick's grandparents, parents and his sister were married. Afterward we're going to throw a big party for all our friends, plus a great many people from the town."

"The party will be on the grounds of my grandparents' farm," Nick said, speaking for the first time. "We've arranged for it to be held beneath a giant tent, so we won't have to worry about the weather."

"And we're going to have a fantastic band," Tess said, continuing where Nick had left off. "There'll also be lots of fabulous food and drinks."

"And in the center of the tent," Nick said, "there'll be

a large, very impressive stack of gold with a sign below it saying there's much more to come.''

Tess slipped her arm around his waist. He slid his arm around her shoulders. "And the best part of it will be that Nick's grandparents will be able to attend. And you, too, Uncle William.''

He nodded. "I'll be there, even if I have to bring my doctor to do it. You can count on me, honey.''

"Good, because I think you're really going to enjoy meeting Nick's grandparents, especially his grandfather. I think you two will have a lot in common. And he'll need special medical arrangements, too.''

"I'll look forward to meeting him.''

Des smiled at her and Nick. "Sounds like a wonderful occasion. I wouldn't miss it.''

"And I'll be there, too,'' Jill said quickly as soon as she heard Des's acceptance.

With a look of irritation at Jill, Kit shifted her stance. "I suppose I will be, too.''

"That's great,'' Tess said brightly, "because I want you two to be my bridesmaids.''

"Excuse me?'' Jill asked, clearly astonished.

"You're my sisters, and I can't think of any one else I would want more than you two to be by my side on the happiest day of my life.''

"You're kidding, right?'' Kit asked.

"Not one bit. So will you?''

Jill looked distinctly shell-shocked. "I—I don't know.''

"Oh, sure you will,'' Des said with a smile at her. "I know you wouldn't want to disappoint your sister, would you?''

"Uh, no, I guess not.''

Kit's expression was distrustful. "Don't think for one

minute I'm going to wear one of those silly, odd-colored dresses with all the frills and ruffles.''

Tess laughed. ''I would never do that to you. We'll go shopping together, and you can pick out whatever you like.''

''Shopping together?'' Kit glanced at Jill, who still looked shell-shocked.

''In fact, we'll take Jill with us,'' Tess said, thoroughly enjoying herself. She knew this was only one step in getting closer to her sisters, but she was so happy, she was overflowing with optimism. ''Jill has excellent taste. We'll all buy our dresses at the same time.''

''I wouldn't miss this for the world,'' Des murmured.

Uncle William held out his hand to Nick. ''Congratulations, young man. You're getting a wonderful girl.''

Nick shook his hand. ''Thank you, sir.'' Then he looked at Tess, tenderness and love etched in his expression and glowing in his eyes. In fact, all the sunshine and brightness that flooded through the windows and into the room seemed concentrated on him, and because he was holding her against him, on her, too. ''All my life I've been looking for treasure, and now, at last, I've found it.''

\* \* \* \* \*

*Look for* THE BARONS OF TEXAS: JILL,
*coming in 2000,*
*only from Silhouette Desire.*

### THE FORTUNES OF TEXAS

*Membership in this family has its privileges
…and its price.
But what a fortune can't buy,
a true-bred Texas love is sure to bring!*

**Coming in October 1999…**

# The Baby Pursuit

by

# LAURIE PAIGE

When the newest Fortune heir was kidnapped, the
prominent family turned to Devin Kincaid to find the
missing baby. The dedicated FBI agent never expected
his investigation might lead him to the altar with
society princess Vanessa Fortune.…

**THE FORTUNES OF TEXAS** continues with
**Expecting… In Texas** by **Marie Ferrarella**,
available in November 1999 from
Silhouette Books.

Available at your favorite retail outlet.

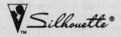

Look us up on-line at: http://www.romance.net          PSFOT2

If you enjoyed what you just read,
then we've got an offer you can't resist!

# Take 2 bestselling love stories FREE!

# Plus get a FREE surprise gift!

**Coming this September 1999
from SILHOUETTE BOOKS
and bestselling author**

# RACHEL LEE

# CONARD COUNTY:

## Boots & Badges

Alicia Dreyfus—a desperate woman on the run—
is about to discover that she *can* come home
again…to Conard County. Along the way she
meets the man of her dreams—and brings together
three other couples, whose love blossoms beneath
the bold Wyoming sky.

Enjoy four complete, **brand-new** stories in one
extraordinary volume.

Available at your favorite retail outlet.

# SILHOUETTE BOOKS
## is proud to announce the arrival of

## THE BABY OF THE MONTH CLUB:

the latest installment of author
**Marie Ferrarella's**
popular miniseries.

When pregnant Juliette St. Claire met Gabriel Saldana
than she discovered he wasn't the struggling artist he
claimed to be. An undercover agent, Gabriel had been
sent to Juliette's gallery to nab his prime suspect: Juliette
herself. But when he discovered her innocence, would he
win back Juliette's heart and convince her that he was the
daddy her baby needed?

*Don't miss Juliette's induction into*
**THE BABY OF THE MONTH CLUB**
*in September 1999.*
Available at your favorite retail outlet.

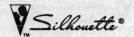

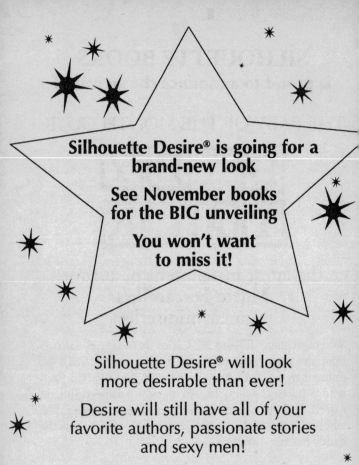

**Silhouette Desire® is going for a brand-new look**

**See November books for the BIG unveiling**

**You won't want to miss it!**

Silhouette Desire® will look more desirable than ever!

Desire will still have all of your favorite authors, passionate stories and sexy men!

On sale at your favorite retailer in October 1999.

 *Silhouette*®

Visit us at: www.romance.net

SDLOOK